ONDER DELIGOZ

LOVE AFTER YOU HAVE GONE

Designed, Published and Distributed by Bookcity.Co

Translated by Stuart Kline

Bookcity.Co

ISBN: 978-1-912311-08-8

To my lovely friend Muj... and
to journalists in jail or in exile

*

I was anxious. Like a wine bottle waiting to be kicked to smithereens in the mosque courtyard. When in fact, I preferred to sleep in the bosom of a drunkard. Neither the ruler of life and death would have come to mind, nor could I have lived with the fear of being shattered to bits with the kick of a pious Moslem.

If only I had the privilege of choosing which one…

Who's guilty now?

*

02:35 AM

I collapsed at the foot of a high street department store door. My turbid mind was busy seeking the answer to the question "who's guilty, motherfucker?" Meanwhile, my eyes caught on a spot two meters away. My stomach churned from the scene I saw half-assed. Great but I had vomited there! Was I supposed to look at my own barf and throw up again? It was as if my gut was in my mouth. My teeth were on the verge of disintegrating and snapping out of my face had I gagged. Actually, vomiting thoroughly and upchucking whatever was inside me would have relaxed me as much as repenting! I don't recall how many pints of beer I downed. Or how many shots of tequila I belted down... Remarkably, I clearly remember the two chaser glasses of rakı. This nausea, this throbbing headache… My God, what a serious pain in the ass! For fuck's sake! As it was, I was up to my neck in enough shit…

I tried to pull myself together but couldn't get to my feet. I was no different from paraplegics with no control over their limbs. I thanked the Almighty my heart was still beating. I forgot my problems that got me into this situation as I was afraid of wetting my pants. Of course, that much beer wasn't going to stay put in me for long. I would've been a total disgrace had I unconsciously pissed in my pants. I remembered the day I peed my pants in elementary school, my legs were all sticky, and I had to wander around school for hours smelling like ammonia. Then I got a rash and had to walk like a newly circumcised kid for a week. I wasn't about to put up with that shit at this age, which is why I needed some urgent help.

I was barely able to make out some blurry figures scurrying behind me on the avenue. I didn't give a damn about them. Wasn't there even a single goddamned soul amongst this crowd willing to grab me by the hand and pull me to my feet? Nope, I guess not. It's not going to happen. What goes around, comes around, dude, what goes around, comes around!

You remember the drunk in the minibus, right? It was also late at night one night about ten years ago. Some guy who was drunk as a skunk got on the minibus. In no shape to stay on his feet, he teetered every which way and was able to open the minibus door after some considerable effort.

My attention was drawn to his bushy black moustache the moment the door opened. His black hair was shining like a 100-watt light bulb. It was undoubtedly dyed. The moment I saw the guy, I told myself, "Dude, this guy's a pimp." Whatever the case, it was indelibly etched in the depth of my mind that everyone who had a bushy moustache and hair dyed pitch black was a pimp. I learned that from the neighborhood punks who'd get a kick out of telling each other exaggerated stories of their whorehouse adventures on street corners. No doubt the guy with the bushy moustache who approached me as I walked down the side street next to the Marmara Hotel, trying to pimp bitches contributed greatly to that indelible stamp. His hair was also dyed and had a beer gut as well. He also had a mouth and a nose. The drunk on the minibus was quite possibly a real pimp. Besides, what difference did it make, he was so tanked, he needed help standing on his own two feet. Well, it was exactly that sort of help I needed right now…

I gave the bushy moustached drunk a derisive look as he gestured he was about to disembark from the minibus. That's when his back crashed to the ground, and his head smacked hard as his legs were left dangling from the minibus steps. He flapped around like an upside-down tortoise. We made eye contact. He reached out his hand, thinking I would lift him out of his desperate predicament. He looked pathetic! How in the hell could I have held that filthy hand? It was smeared with barf, totally disgusting! The filthy drunk would be better off dead. Anyways, not everyone on the minibus didn't share my thinking. Two folks sitting in the front seat helped out the poor slob. Yes, I didn't entertain such thoughts that day, but the guy with the shiny black hair and coarse moustache was pathetic. I swear to God I'm going to scream if I wasn't so ashamed; "Motherfuck, I'm even more pathetic than that drunk I didn't aid!" In reality, nobody would give a shit if I was ashamed, as there was no way I could finish a sentence with this inebriated head of mine, nor did I have the strength to scream.

02:41 AM

- Are you alright?

- Hı hııı…

You walked away from the scene. Is that all the sensibility you've got? You thought I was okay just because I said "Hı hııı"? You could've lent me a hand, bitch, were you a guy or a broad? Maybe you were a trannie. Your thick voice was cause for concern. You were fine whatever you were, man… Your beauty flowed into me from between my eyelashes I was only able to pry half open. I hope to fuck's sake you aren't one of those wanting to look like a broad. I wouldn't want some trannie to be getting me all excited now, would I! Frankly, I'm afraid of them. It was only last night when a transvestite scared the shit out of me. I still can't figure out how they sudden multiplied mushroom-like in our district, famous for its staunch fundamentalist stance. That day, I'd gone to Esenler, where I'd spent my childhood. After having my tenant pay me two months of accumulated rent, I got caught up in a long chat with some old friends of mine, and it was quite late when I made it back home. I had gotten off the city bus and was walking calmly, headlong down the street towards my home. I was wearing leather-soled, eggplant-purple shoes. My belt was of the same purple hue, but it had nothing to with what happened to me.

The butcher with a beard, a religious head cap and big belly – it might be a beer gut – who sold his uncle's fresh-plucked chickens, the herbalist, who sold dusty packages of spices atop musty-smelling shelves, the corner shopkeeper who filled the bellies of bachelor construction workers with salami and cheese sandwiches. Then there were the Urfa- and Diyarbakır-kebap shops lined up from end to end towards the bottom of the street. Various dreams climbed along a cul-de-sac that turned off on the right side to a steeply inclined street. A woman was washing down her balcony. Runoff water poured from the cul-de-sac down from to the gutter on the main avenue. I noticed the soapy water, but my mind was on the cul-de-sac. The transvestites' flats were on that street. I mumbled to myself, "How was it they were able to move into this neighborhood" as the pain in my buttocks brought tears to my eyes. The water pouring from the cul-de-sac became a skating rink beneath my crappy leather-soled shoes, causing me to slip and fall on my ass. I yelled

"Ahhh" out loud. I thought the entire neighborhood would be in an uproar but not a sound was heard from anybody. Fuck, not even a curtain moved in one of the windows I peeked into from below. Forget the house folks, not even the barber Serhat, whom I mentioned to friends and family was "a lousy barber, but was a very decent guy," stuck his head out from his door. No doubt he was filling out lottery tickets. What else could he be doing at that hour?

Wait a sec, what was it that reminded me of my pain in the butt? Yeah, it was the transsexual. You can call it a transvestite. Call it whatever you want, it's your humanity. Well, a voice came from the source of the water that made me fall on my ass that night. I was still writhing on the ground from my hurt butt. The voice I heard was neither male nor female. I can't describe it, but it had a tone characteristic of transvestites. The voice was a bit rough around the edges, yet it asked with a gentleness rarely encountered in these parts, "Speedy recovery, Are you alright, do you need any help?" It had addressed me formally. I had lived in that neighborhood for years, and I never heard a single shopkeeper or neighbor address me in a formal tone. When in fact I was sensitive on this matter. I even addressed the kid with a fresh moustache selling stuffed mussels on the street corner formally. Of course, even that burro would have left my sensibility of mine unrequited every time. Whaddya mean respect? The asshole was only worried about how fast he could thrust my money in his pocket as if he wanted to stuff my mouth with mussels with their shells in his tray. While my hangup about formality loomed so large, it may have been the pain in my ass that triggered my inertly rude response to the owner of the gentle manner who asked about my condition. I couldn't respond, let alone look in his/her face. I only noticed his curly black hair that shined whenever light hit it was as every bit as black and shiny as the dyed hair of the drunk of that indelibly stamped pimp on the minibus. Yeah, but this was a tranny. This similarity further diluted my mind that writhed at the foot of the door. Was coal-black hair the reason for disregarding both the drunk oaf who tried boarding the minibus and the trannie? One wanted help while the other wanted to help.

- What are you saying, dude, don't fuck with me...

I instantly remembered my name. Frankly speaking, I was running a self-check to see if I could recall, just as I always did during my drunken spells. You know, they removed İstiklal's cobblestone pavements and replaced them with soulless pieces of concrete, right? Well, I always made the connecting lines of the concrete blocks my walking path and check to see whether I was walking straight or not. Because I drank a couple draughts of beer most of the time, I would pass both tests in grand style and be happy. Forget about walking along a straight line. I can't even get up from the spot where I've fallen. I could only remember my name this time. My name's Sitki. Sidkullah. Forgive me Allah!

02:55 AM

-Hey, girl, are you nuts, what are you doing with that drunken fool, just look at him, he's down and out, Fuck, the bitch threw up too, let's just get the fuck outta here.

- Wait a sec, girl, hey, did you ever see a manicured drunk?

What the fuck? How about that? Even if I was straight, I'd never be able to make out a manicure in this darkness, how'd you see that shit, girl? As she had such a hang up about manicures, I bet she was one of those women who bites her nails and destroys her cuticles. I was able to pry my eyes open just a bit to better understand the broad towering over me, examining me like a cadaver. I looked her over from head to foot as much as I was able to look her over. I couldn't quite make out what she had on, whether she had Converse on her feet, or wearing black jeans or stretch tights. I was surprised as my eyes slid upwards. She was wearing a dress that stretched practically down to her knees over her jeans. I was still wasn't sure whether she was wearing tights or not underneath. Why was this girl's head covered on a summer's day? That's a headscarf, idiot! What time is it, by the way? Was it morning? What is this girl doing here at this hour?

This broad who had callously gotten right up next to me to the heavy alcohol stench must have understood the part of my mumbling about the time, she replied by saying "It's three thirty, dude." I heard a voice two steps away that was as grating as chalk being scraped over s blackboard. "Girl, what the hell do you care about what time it is!" I tried bulging my eyes to look in the direction where the voice came from. Facing me was a girl with her arms folded across her chest and hunched over. I immediately made out her pointed teeth gushing out from her upper lip. Her hair was also in a mess. She wore a white T-shirt over blue jeans, and colorful laced sports shoes on her feet. She was just one of those types who hung out in the neighborhood with sloppy clothing morning noon and night. Great but why did this toothy bitch get so uptight when she heard what time it was? You fucking cunt, if you were so worried about the time, what are you doing on the street at this hour? You're just like the spinster girls who go home with the evening call to prayer. What a phony! I'm a monkey's uncle if she's not a girl who knows venues where they play good music and serve cheap brew. I'm also a monkey's uncle if she doesn't know all the side streets in

Beyoğlu, at least the roads, places to take shelter to resort to in times of trouble and the most swaggering foul language to counter harassment. I was peeved at first glance, but now I liked this girl. I liked her foul-mouthed style. Dude, cussing is the Swiss Army knife of all turbulent lives and dilemma souls. It calms people down, it wipes their tears, it comforts them, makes them happy. As it is, those with foul mouths only harm themselves.

While I was checking out the faraway girl, the broad looming over me was getting a bit carried away. I felt her breath on my face. It was warm enough to make we want to forget about my fucked up stomach and press my lips against hers. But I didn't make the attempt. I was afraid I'd miss her lips and suck her nose instead. My eyes slid back to her dress hanging over her pants. A light was blinking in her pocket. Before I had the chance to mumble anything, the girl two steps away yelled, "There's a light in your pocket, a light! Your phone's ringing, girl, why don't you answer it?" Meanwhile, I understood the problem of the broad towering over me. She was looking at my book stuck between my head and the wall. Without giving me the chance to say, "Take it if you want, I finished it before I got drunk," she reached down and picked it up. As she lifted the book cover of the book, her friend got all vamp-like. "C'mon girl, I still have to get to Esenler, Melihat's going to get really pissed at me! Hey, your phone is on silent, but don't tell me you don't notice the light?"

The girl towering over me must have sensed what I was thinking as she stuck the book under her armpit. While I wished her happiness with Oblomov, she removed her cell phone from her pocket. Before answering her telephone, she snarled at her friend, "Don't you ever call your mother by her name, Zahide or else I'll fuck you up." It was understood the toothy girl didn't like her mother very much. It was obvious when she said, "Fuck it, Melihat, answer it already." The broad standing over me answered her phone, "Okay, man, we'll be in front of The Marmara in five minutes, pick us up from there," then hung up the phone. Zahide turned her back and began to saunter off. Without paying her any heed, the girl towering over grabbed a pen from her purse. She leaned over and wrote something on my right hand. I felt tingly as the tip of her pen wrote a lap around my palm. "I'll return your book after I read it, and you can call me once you sober up, okay?" Then she ran off to catch up to her friend.

Who the fuck are these freaks, who'd pick them up at this hour? I looked carefully from behind before they disappeared into the darkness. The girl who loomed over me had a huge camera hanging off her shoulder. The camera was swinging to and fro as she ran. So, she was a girl photographer wearing a headscarf. Dude, I was either dreaming or else the country's only headscarved midnight photographer was standing over me. They just made me continually repeat the word 'light' and disappeared into the darkness.

03:11 AM

-Light, light, lightttt, much mooore light, hope, hope hopee, much mooore hope.

Dozing behind half-opened eyelids, my eyes bulged. I was forcing my eyelids not to descend into total darkness. I had seen the light in the pocket of the headscarved midnight photographer. The toothy girl behind her said light. The alcohol meandering in my veins was so concentrated that my eyelids gave up the fight and were out for the count. But that chorus had crescendoed upon my drunken tongue big time. I might've forgotten my way home, I might've forgotten my name; my mind might've become so blurry to the extent that I might not have found my mouth while drinking water, but it would've been practically impossible for me to forget that chorus. I wasn't giving up even though the words spewed half-assed out of my mouth. I'd say, "Light, light, lightttt,

much mooore light, hope, hope hopee, much mooore hope"
then continually rewind the phrase back to the beginning.
As it was, I'd been doing this constantly for the past 15 years.
It had been spinning around my tongue while lying down,
getting up, eating drinking, peeing, fucking and most of
all, collapsing to the ground like lazy dogs while thinking;"
Light, light, lightttt, much mooore light, hope, hope hopee,
much mooore hope."

1996 was coming to an end, and those taking part in
New Year's parties that were broadcast live from expensive
hotels and decked-out television studios were joyfully ringing
in 1997. I was at my flat that was situated in a neighborhood
surrounded by apartment complexes up above and a ghetto
down below. That night, I was in the class of those ringing
in the New Year in front of the TV. I had leaned back on the
la-z-boy of the living room ensemble that we purchased two
weeks ago from the 20-m2 Hakkı Shopping Center located
in the neighborhood square, shoehorned between the
propane tank shop and jewellery shop and somehow didn't
have the guts to sit on it as a family. After rocking my three-
year-old sister to sleep at her foot, my mother, who couldn't
bear having the kid on the sofa for fear of premature wear,
was stretched out on a floor cushion, continually snarled at
me to sit up straight. She was expecting loyalty from me,
a kid who posed in front of the mirror with brilliantine-
shaped hair at least 17 times a day, my zits that cover my
entire face and eyes, and who has suddenly plunged into
puberty with sex dreams at any moment. Having named

me 'Sıdkullah,' she assumed I was going to remain loyal to my character. After fighting tooth-and-nail morning, noon and persuading my father in bed sweet talking incessantly from night until morning for two months straight, she just couldn't bring herself to sit on the ensemble after it arrived in our home. She didn't want it to be worn out so quickly. Even sitting on the floor and leaning her back against the new armchairs meant great comfort for my mother. She could've been right with this sensitivity regarding the future of her sofa set with her chubby cheeks, breasts larger than her head and a belly that expanded five-fold whenever she sat down. After putting my sister to bed, she began munching on sunflower seeds. Meanwhile, she slammed me for changing the channel so often. "Hey, just stop on a channel for a bit, you're making me dizzy," so I promptly got stuck on one of the channels. Actually, I quit zapping because I liked the images that flowed on the screen. While everyone was having a blast at parties, nightclubs and hotels, I was spending New Year's Eve with a father who was snoring next to the stove and a chubby mother who couldn't even make a tiny cake and was eating huge pumpkin seeds. I was bummed out and getting fed up with indiscriminately pressing the buttons on the remote. I patiently watched skits that made me mutter under my breath, "Screw your thought-provoking bullshit humor that's supposed to make us laugh, and special New Year's shows staged by famous theatrical stars that are fobbed onto viewers. Afterwards, there was a long commercial break; I couldn't bear them any longer and picked up the remote, its button lettering worn off from being pressed all the time. I forced a button that had its "p+" lettering worn off completely and only worked by pressing on it with my fingernail edge. My effort was rewarded with a song that I wouldn't stop singing for years to come. I was watching one of nation's first private channels. Guaranteed to leave its rivals in the rating dust, this station had the nation's most popular popstar sing its New Year's song. It was Tarkan who was singing. He still hadn't ventured abroad to become a superstar with his hit album in English. That said, it was a time when he was at the top of the national charts while girls swooned 'Tarkaaannnn' at the top of their lungs at his concerts throughout the country. It was still back at the time when Tarkan launched each of his albums with a different image, paving the way for several envious copycat artists to claw their way up the charts in his wake, something he most probably got a big kick out of. So, there he was, calmly singing in the New Year.

"Little angels split this morning's darkness

Dawn fell sweetly, dawn fell sweetly

It was very pleasant to awake to the realities today

Light, light, lighttt, much mooore light,

Hope, hope hopee, much mooore hope

Let the New Year renew us once again

It's the only harbinger of our hopes"

I lapsed into entirely different dreams in the armchair where I sat whenever Tarkan hit upon his "light, light lighhht" melody. I contemplated a black-eyed girl who captured my heart when I was a kid. She moved onto our street with her mother, her elder sister and her elder brother.I memorized her every motion starting from the moment our eyes made contact. Every breath she took, every step she took, every situation she got herself into whenever we were apart was indelibly etched upon my mind. Right on up until our final encounter. We rendezvoused with my childhood love on the terrace of our neighbor from Samsun one evening in August. Neither of us knew it was to be the final time together. How could we have known that fate was going to toss us into a scenario worse than 'True Romance?' There was no way of knowing that sweet romanticism was going to be shot up amongst characters and events straight out of a Tarantino movie. I mean, we were happy and hopeful that our happiness would continue. My black-eyed petite amour told me "You are my hope." I replied spontaneously "You're my light." I don't have a notion how that came into my mind… Now was this song of Tarkan's a coincidence or a divine message? I hadn't a clue. While I listened to the tune and dwelled in the melancholy, I recalled our last date with my Hatice and began murmuring "Where are you, my light. "Where are you, my light."

Hatice's arrival...

Hatice was from Diyarbakir, in southeastern Turkey. It would have been a sheer lie to say she was happy that summer. It was June 1993 when she arrived in the big city. But she would end up longing for the last winter she spent in Diyarbakir. The temperature was still cold and all the colors ranged between black and white. She viewed her hometown of Silvan, a provincial district of Diyarbakir, as colorful and peaceful as paradise. Though she never saw the provincial center, the city was hers, the provincial district was hers, the neighborhood was hers, the street was hers as was her home. Her mother Munise, her elder brother Abdurrahman and her elder sister Leyla were always beside her. But once spring arrived, things got rather turbulent in Silvan. The sound of gunfire she became familiar with at weddings where her braided hair swung to and fro amidst the skirts of folk-dancing women reverberated throughout the provincial district practically every night. During the winter's bleakest days, her mother, brother and sister began whispering to each other in remote corners. They kept repeating to themselves, "Let's not stick around very much in these parts. Let's have the girl finish school, then we can get out of here." In addition to the darkness spreading gradually in the district, it was the neighborhood peer pressure that really did her mother Munise in. Yılmaz, the son of brother-in-law, was sought by the authorities at the time. It was said he had aided the PKK, which fired on a police station at the foot of the mountain. However, Munise was not made aware of such activities. Had she known he had really aided and abetted the PKK, she wouldn't have let Yılmaz into the garden, let alone the house. Regardless of the case, weapons and death weren't her cup of tea… She'd always say, "Why take the life that Allah has given?" Of course, those who called on Yılmaz didn't care what Aunt Munise was thinking. They frequently came knocking on Munise's door in their civilian clothes. A startled Munise would tremble whenever the white Renault Toros pulled up next to her garden gate. The charged into the house with their stern looks, without saying a work, without any greetings, and without waiting to be asked inside, wasting no time in searching the place with a fine-tooth comb. With their frequent raids, they had already committed to memory each and every remote corner of the home. To the extent of being able to place and remove the soap-scented clean bed sheets from the wooden cabinet next to the mattresses had they wanted to sleep over. The entire civilian search team knew the color of the embroidered doilies stored in Munise's dowry chest, the place where her husband Remzi's watch was kept, and the cassettes that Leyla kept in her clothes cabinet. They also know that nothing of note would turn up from their run-of-the mill rummage party. The objective was to scare, that's all. It wasn't the fear of death, but rather civilians entering the abode wearing their shoes, something that ired Munise to no end. She wanted to ask them every time they came stomping in, "Don't your mothers perform their daily prayers, fellas?" No doubt, it was the heart-in-the-mouth fear warning her every time that she needed to remain quiet now so she'd be able to speak later on. Munise ended up moaning and groaning as she cleaned the carpets after each house search.

The civil security forces came knocking on Munise's door again on a winter's day. This time around, there were four of them as they came trouncing into the home with their shoes again. They tracked their muddy shoes on the carpets Munise had washed by hand just two weeks ago. Once again, the house folk retreated into the wall recesses in their perturbed state. Leyla, beneath the triangle shelf in the corner of the living room, Abdurrahman in the opposite corner, and Munise standing guard at the foot of the door. Hatice's spot was the same once again, affixing herself to her mother's belly like a baby kangaroo. A desperate mother and her three kids, patiently watching the civilians trash their household… If they didn't leave immediately, it would take until midnight to clean the house all over again and put the things back in their place. They didn't leave and they turned the place upside down. They even turned the pages of the Quran on the wall one by one, their dirty hands leaving indelible stains on the yellow pages ornamented with verses. There was also indelible fear, their hearts skipping a beat or two …

One of the civilians suddenly turned on Abdurrahman like a swarm of locusts, yelling, "Are you a member of the organization too, punk?" At the moment, Munise gasped for air. She didn't know Turkish but she knew this sentence and the persecution it bore within very well. Racing beneath her white-flowered purple flannel dress, her heart was pumping fear instead of blood. What if they take away her only son, believing he was a member of the organization? Then what if he doesn't come back? At least her husband Remzi, who died in a construction accident, has a grave. What would happen if Abdurrahman left and didn't return? Would she be saddened by Abdurrahman's absence or for the fact he didn't even have a gravestone to grieve at? The whirlpool overwhelming Abdurrahman was no different from that of his mother. He was petrified. He was barely able to say to the interrogating civilian, "No, I swear on the Quran, no!" in a quavering voice. Actually, the civilians knew damn well that Abdurrahman had nothing to do with that business. They were just screwing around with him and they managed to scare the dickens out of him. Well, that was the day Munise decided to pull up stakes she put off for so long and leave the place she called home.

The most somber tone of gray enveloped Hatice's neighborhood as summer approached. The sounds of reverberating gunshots heard after midnight became a nightmare for Hatice. There was a cabinet right next to her bed where guest blankets and mattresses were kept. Hatice squeezed herself between her bed and the cabinet on those noisy nights. Like refugees fleeing a war zone, she took refuge in this safe zone every night. As the gun shots echoed, she experienced anxiety attacks, worried sick if anything happened to her mother, or if she was alive or not. Regardless of whether her tongue and palate were dry from constant gulping, or whether she was afraid of having to get up at six in the morning in order to go to school, she would drift off to sleep. Actually, there were nights when she would resist sleeping in order not to have nightmares. She no longer had the dreams like she had when she was little when she'd say to her mother, "I had a really nice dream, lie next to me and I'll tell you about it if you want." After a few hours of sleep, she'd wake up in the morning with bloodshot eyes. Each and every day that began following those lead-heavy nights, she'd witness the plans put forward by her elders of them moving to a faraway place. They weren't aware, but Hatice knew quite well what they were secretly talking about. She was quite sad knowing the time to abandon their homes would coincide with the day she received her report card. She said inwardly, "I wonder if we won't go if I fail my class?" Sometimes she gave credit to her elders, especially as they had begun to fear living on the land they were born. She was a high-school sophomore at the age of 14 and words that turned the array of bright colors of her native land from paradise to a grayish hell were at the center of her life. 'Guerilla,' 'terrorist,' 'organization,' 'unsolved murder,' 'execution,' 'bullets,' 'operation'… She became familiar with these heart-stopping words from both her elders whispering in the nooks and crannies, as well as the deep conversations she engaged with her classmates on the way to school.

They used to sing folk songs, laugh and chase each other about on the road to school. As the lifeline of the children in the provincial district changed, so did their road. They were now accompanied by somber stories of death they heard from their circles. With each story, the road that twisted between the rows of poplar trees to the right and left was turning into a tunnel of fear their peers in the big cities paid money to enter at amusement parks. In fact, theirs was much worse than those tunnels that spread terror in exchange for money in that the road was free and the stories were real. Such was the case that little kids of the poplar-lined road had also disappeared. They used to make gun barrels with their pointer fingers and hide behind the trees, aiming at each other as they imitated the sound of gunshots, 'tak u rak'. Some of them pronounced this with the letter 'r' with their small, sweet tongues. There was a noticeable difference between the interjections of 'tak u yak' emerging from the fingertip barrels and the 'tak u rak' sounds that came from behind the opposite poplar tree. They all disappeared in the end. The chirpy 'tak u rak' on the tongues of children who opened one of their hands widely to say their age mixed with the night to became the sound of bullets fired from steel barrels. They assumed 'ah's in the bodies they pierced, turning to blood which spattered on the ground. The kids started playing games that didn't force them to say 'tak u rak' in front of their mothers. It wasn't much, but they learned that they always needed to be within arm's reach if the 'tak u rak's were heard in the morning in order to take shelter in their mothers' embrace. They didn't even hide behind the poplar trees.

The scene was always the same when they arrived at school. Boys who'd never quit playing soccer even into the world turned to ashes were running to and fro in sweaty abandonment in the grey school bungalow's long, narrow concrete playground. They kicked the plastic ball breathlessly, trying to get it to go between two rocks. Above all, they'd dance the Macarena whenever the ball passed through the goalie's leg, as their choice obscenities aimed at the goalie's integrity and chortling reverberated off the cracked concrete. Matches in which boys ended up with banged-up knees and bloody elbows were held with plenty of fierce mid-field struggling and treachery around the goalposts. As per the agreement made at the start of play, each kid that assumed the goalie position in turn wanted to eat three goals as soon as possible because they dreamed of returning to the pitch as goal king Tanju or the devil Rıdvan. They liked it when the ball ended up in their own goalposts, as they tried to prevent the goal with fake moves. Some sly dogs would be subject to some serious ass chewing when they charged offensively but didn't help out with the defense at all.

While the boys were booting the ball around, the girls were either strolling about the playground in groups or else in every nook and cranny putting their heads together and chatting. They eyed the pipsqueak boys with white clouds of sweat seeping through their tank-tops to crystallize on their blue shirts, giggling as they matched them to each other. Nevertheless, after all their grinning and sweet gossip they gaped at the pipsqueak boys with white clouds of sweat seeping through their tank-tops to crystallize on their blue shirts, they'd always drop anchor in the same harbor of fear and the same situation. These were students whose equal lack of assets was immediately apparent whenever one of the kids polished their shoes. They lacked plenty and had nothing that was complete, their lives equalized in poverty. Sometimes equality was not fair at all. What made it all the more excruciatingly painful was the fact their fears were now on an equal footing.

For Hatice, June arrived much sooner than previous years. The second week of the month was also ending. The scene in the school playground hadn't changed. Buckethead Mustafa had the ball in front of him and was knocking aside everyone who got in his way. None of the pipsqueaks who had tumbled to the ground protested Buckethead Mustafa's actions. Buckethead Mustafa was twice as wide and 50% taller than his peers and had a body that was 100% bigger than some of them. He was the first pick for these matches, not so much for his ball driving technique, but for his girth. As it was, he'd beat the daylights out of those who didn't pick him first. Actually, Buckethead Mustafa's inner world was in opposite proportion to his burliness. He had such finesse to the extent that he once donned his sister's heeled slippers and tried walking in them like a model taking the podium. If only his feet were as fine as his soul. Had that been the case, the sides of his newly-engaged sister's slippers with pink feathers on top might not have blown out. Buckethead Mustafa suffered so much as to want to deeply bury the tides of his soul when he tied the slippers to a rock and tossed them down the well behind the house so that nobody would see them. Inasmuch as living was becoming difficult at school in one mode, at home in another mode and in his inner world in a completely different mode. While he was fragile in his solitary world as the meaning of his surname 'Narin', transforming into his abusive Buckethead Mustafa in crowds began to wear down his zigzagging psychology.

Having removed the dark eyebrow hairs right above his nose with his sister's tweezers before he left home in the morning, Buckethead Mustafa transformed into the meanest, toughest kid of the concrete playground when he reached school. Everyone assumed he was playing ball. However, he was merely playing the role of Buckethead Mustafa. Finally, he ground to a halt when the school bell rang. It was to be the final bell that summoned the pupils to class. It was report card time.

The homeroom teacher thrust the report card with its fresh paper smell and embellished with the trite phrase "I wish you continued success" into Hatice's hand as if to say "Your time's come, get outta here." Hatice received a '6' in Geography and '10's in all her other subjects. Her Geography teacher graduated recently, didn't speak much, very sullen, a bit handsome and rather repugnant. His name was Erkan. Though he didn't have a droopy beard like the Seljuq Emperor Alparslan in the picture hanging on the school wall, he was known as a beardless member of the political movement in the neighborhood called "We've got no other friends other than ourselves." According to widespread belief, he gave low grades to all students who didn't enter the friend class because he was a Kurd. If only the geography teacher was a supporter of Özal, like her mother and brother had been. President Turgut Özal, who was the chairman of the honeycomb party, had passed away just last month. Her mother Munise had loved Özal ever since he was the prime minister, was greatly saddened by his passing. She even cried. Had Geography Teacher Erkan thought like Munise, he might've given her the grade she deserved. Anyways, she still received a certificate of merit. However, this time it was filled with melancholy. She wasn't going to skip gaily down the school road like she did last year. She wasn't going to raise her certificate of merit in the air the moment she entered their garden and shout out to her sister, "Look what I got!" She didn't feel like it. Her brother Abdurrahman wasn't going to pet her hair and say, "Bravo, dark girl," then pick up a hammer and thrust the certificate of merit onto the nail he banged into the wall. Everyone was thinking about migrating. Preparations didn't take long as there were just two spring mattresses and a few pieces of furniture in their home. The largest loads were the floor beds and cushions.

It was Sunday morning when a green truck pulled up in front of the home. There was an odd gap showing the opposite side when looking from the side in the center spot of the truck's long nose. It also emitted a 'dizzit' sound every 15-20 meters. Everyone in the provincial district called it the 'dizzit' truck, instantly recognizing its sound even as it passed through the rear neighborhood. It belonged to pot-bellied Bahattin, whose thick moustache grew into his mouth. Bahattin was a burly guy, but his wife Saniye was even burlier than him. She was a foul-mouthed woman, and would jump in Bahattin's shit whenever she didn't get her way. Strutting around like a redneck outside, Bahattin floated about like a fresh damsel in the presence of his wife the house. This closet henpecked Bahattin was so sick of his wife's bitching, he was thrilled beyond words whenever he got a long-haul job. He'd return to Silvan as late at night as possible. He enjoyed spending time at truckers' restaurants, roadside whorehouses and taverns. Most of the time, instead of sleeping in the bosom of Saniye, with her boobs sagging down to her waist, he preferred banging a whore he haggled over on the side of the road in his truck cab. In short, the longer the haul, Bahattin's revenge on his bitchy wife became all the more sweeter and longer lasting.

A "Movers 'R Us" sign written in lopsided letters was hanging in the dizzit truck's windshield. The dizzit truck was going to move Hatice's home now. On one side, neighbors and relatives were shedding tears while on the other side, their worldly possessions were being loaded into the dizzit truck. Every word spilling from their mouths echoed in the now vacant home. Every sound that reverberated off the walls was steeped in anguish. Every sorrow pierced their hearts like lances and opened deep voids in Munise, Leyla and the little girl of the house, Hatice. Plenty of memories seeped into those voids to settle into the deepest recesses of their hearts. So they would constantly be remembered, so the tears of a mother and her two daughters would never dry. Memories didn't merely knock on Abdurrahman's heart door. He had sealed his heart off from Silvan long ago. He didn't even pack a single momento into his suitcase that would make him laugh away the melancholy.

One by one, Hatice had taken her report cards and merit certificates off the wall and placed them in her bag the night before. She pitched in the moving effort as she picked up small items and carried them out to the truck. On her way out from the house to the truck, friends and relatives pulled her by the arm, kissing and hugging her as dirges were sung. Every time she went out to the truck, she thought, "I had no idea I was loved so much." In essence, she was loved, but there was an underlying reason for all her friends' and relatives' wailing dirges. There was a palpable fear running through their community, whereas they were lamenting for the unbearable situation they found themselves in as well. Everyone had their own problems and blew off temporary steam by lamenting. Hatice's biggest problem was her father. How was he going to leave that bullet-riddled land behind? What soil was she going to touch whenever she wanted to visit the grave she considered as her father's? Would she be able to find soil in the big city? Her father Remzi moved to Istanbul when she was just six months old. He went for work in order for his wife and children's welfare. One day, he fell from the top of the construction job site onto a stack of bricks on the ground. He was pulling bricks onto the 12th floor when his hand got caught in the pulley, forcing him to lose his balance and fall fatally to the ground. The young man who went far from home with a wooden suitcase returned in a wooden casket in the baggage compartment of a bus. If Hatice's heart was reeling, it was because they were fleeing to find life in the city where her father gave his life.

It was their turn once all their belongings were carefully positioned into the dizzit truck. She clambered up into the truck cab together with her mother and sister. As their stuff didn't even fill half of the space, there was room to open a floor mattress in the center of the truck bed. A few loaves of bread, tomatoes, cucumbers and some biscuits the neighbors had brought around were all stacked in a corner to eat along the way. Her brother was going to sit in front together with the tall, beefy driver. While they managed to hold back their tears while everything was being loaded, Munise and Leyla couldn't keep from sobbing once the tailgate was locked into place. One was leaving a dead husband while the other was leaving dreams of marrying her sweetheart lad of the home at the top of their street together behind them. The fear of going to a land where they had no idea what to expect ratcheted up their anguish another notch. With the exception of the time they were able to catch some winks, her mother and sister cried the entire journey. The truck made four stops along the way. Hatice was only able to see her brother Abdurrahman during these breaks. Abdurrahman didn't look too worried, as he was mainly concerned with getting the hell outta Silvan. Looks like he got what he wanted.

These stopovers meant new experiences for Hatice. Not counting the festivals, this was the first time she was dining outside her home. With the exception of the çivil servants who came to Silvan, she was seeing people with different faces and languages for the first time. Meanwhile, this was also the first time she paid Money to use the toilet, how embarrassing that was! She ran into a pool for the first time right next to the stopover they made near Bolu. Kids were swimming in it and they looked happy. She was struck by the children who were startled by the whoosh sound made when a chubby bugger dove headfirst into the pool. She laughed as she sighed inwardly, "the sound of bullets in Silvan, and the sound of 'whoosh' here." If only she hadn't ever heard the sound of bullets and was only startled by water ejected by a well-fed kid leaping into a pool.

Munise and Leyla never got out of the truck during the stopovers. If it was up to them, they'd have spent the rest of their lives in the truck bed. The edge of the tarpaulin covering the truck bed was left open so air could get inside. Besides air, the dark truck bed also filled with the music coming from the driver's cab. Henpecked Bahattin had bought İbrahim Tatlıses's latest cassette. He listened into Tatlıses' folk-tunes, turning it over constantly. In fact, most of the time he didn't even play the reverse side, but rather just rewound the 'Ah Keşkem' tüne back to the beginning. Sometimes, the cassette would rewind by itself, which is when Henpecked Bahattin would let rip with a torrent of obscenities. "You son-of-a-…" He generally didn't finish this phrase. First, he'd pulled the truck over to a suitable spot. After carefully removing the spooled cassette from the cassette deck, he'd insert his pinky into the serrated round hole and rewind the spool of tape back to the appropriate place. He could've done this process much quicker had he used a pen instead of his pinky, which barely fit into that space. The moment he pushed the cassette back into the deck and heard the music, he punched the gas pedal and steered the truck back onto the highway. Keşkems were spreading from the cab. Hatice also dug this folk-tune very much as it had a catchy rhythm and cool lyrics. The shrill horn at the beginning of the tune made us feel like we were dancing at a wedding whenever we heard that sound. She poked her head out of the truck bed the moment she heard the 'ah keşkem ah keşkem's filling that tiny space. She wanted to hear the folk tune more clearer. It hadn't been very long since they departed, but the 'ah keşkems' reminded her of the friends she loved so much. The brother of the neighbor girl Süheyla bought Ibrahim Tatlıses' cassette. After he went to work, Süheyla would call Hatice and other friends over. They'd gather in the room with the floor cushions, a family photograph embedded into an outlet border, a Quran hanging on the wall and a cassette deck. They'd stick the cassette in the deck and turn on 'Ah Keşkemi,' which they'd listen to time and time again. Once, Süheyla couldn't resist and asked, "What is 'keşkem'?" Hatice and the other girls were dumbfounded and they were at a loss for words. However, Hatice was able to suggest

"That word is 'keşke' (if only), my dumb friend" sometime later. But Süheyla wasn't convinced and she insisted it had another meaning. She blurted emphatically "What is my keşkem." Hatice was also confused. Together with full string orchestration, İbrahim Tatlıses was singing from the driver's cab:

"If only I could go out with you, if only, if only

If only I could hold your hand, if only, if only

If only I could hug your waist at cafes and discos, if only, if only"

Hatice was curious; "what is 'keşkem'?"

Whenever she felt bored, Hatice would stick her head out from that small space and look around her. She was bidding farewell to her native land with her braided hair airborne in the wind. The dusty, earthen narrow roads had widened sometime behind her and had become entirely asphalt. The apartment buildings were also growing as they progressed. She wasn't one of those kids who counted electricity poles on the side of the road while making a journey. However, she did try counting the number of apartment stories as they passed through city centers. She had a problem in that she wondered how high a 12-storey apartment, was, the height from which her father fell to his death. Her squinting eyes never encountered a 12-storey apartment building. But once she saw an 8-storey building, it wasn't hard for her to imagine what a 12-storey building looked like. Once she recalled the day she fell from the roof of a single-story bungalow and broke her arm, she had felt the terror of the suffering her father experienced since her childhood.

The truck had entered Istanbul without Hatice seeing even a single 12-storey building along the way. She saw huge, crowded roads, and chaotic buildings of all heights. Meanwhile, she could only see blue as she peered from the tarp space. The blue on top was the sky, but what was that below them? She said inwardly, 'If only the truck could pass over the bridge a bit more slowly." She wanted to gaze at the sea, something she saw for the first time in her life. She still wasn't aware of the metropolitan crowds, that could see the Bosphorus while moving to the European side of Istanbul, spending 15-20 years going between work and home in the city's outlying areas without going to seaside even once. Then again, she considered herself lucky on the matter of getting acquainted with the sea. What if the home they moved to had been on the Anatolian side?

The instant they passed over the bridge, Hatice's dark eyes encountered buildings that touched the clouds. As she began breathing in the air of the European continent, she asked, "I wonder which of these buildings was the one that took my father's life?" It was a weak askance, posed to and heard by herself. She wanted to pose this question to her mother, the answer of which couldn't be found for the rest of her life. She suddenly turned her back and decided against posing this question. She didn't want to make her mother any sadder than she was with her swollen eyes purple from weeping. She wasn't going to see her father again, even had she learned all the details. She was never going to embrace her father, who embraced life fully. Just like the sky and sea in the scenery she had just witnessed …

About 20 minutes after crossing the bridge, the truck trundled off the congested freeway at the Esenler Atışalanı exit. After progressing a bit down a wide avenue, it turned into some side streets. Hatice couldn't hold back from saying "So this is the big city!" The scenery spread out before her only served to flame her longing for Silvan. The irregular apartment buildings, the mud-filled streets, the piles of garbage… The truck proceeded slowly on such a street, which seemed to be under total construction. Most of the homes had no mortar on the brick masonry and those that were mortared weren't painted. She said inwardly, "Our home was better than these." Of course, there was the occasional apartment with painted protective balcony bars and tiny ornamental stones on their outer facades. She was going to learn later they were German-Turkish apartments. The dizzit truck came to a stop in front of one such apartment. The building was three-stories high. Good thing it was like that, what if it was 12-stories? Its outer facade was as gaudy as the tapestry hung in their home back in Silvan. She asked in amazement, "How did they stick the tiny stones one by one on that wall?" She wasn't impressed with the embellishment as she was with the trouble that went into that work. The moment she got out of the truck, she asked her brother Abdurrahman, "How do they do that?" Once he responded,

"They're glass mosaic stones, dark girl, they're stuck on in blocks," her amazement instantly dissipated. She planted her eyes on the balconies of the 3-storey German-Turkish apartment without paying any heed to the endearing words of her uncle Halil, who greeted them, as she wondered, "Which floor are we going to live on?" Meanwhile, her mother and sister had descended from the truck and started hastily pouring out their grief with Uncle Halil. She saw folks she didn't recognize moving their belongings from the truck into the flamboyant ground floor of the German-Turkish building. Great, but wasn't this a shop or something like that? That's when her excitement fizzled out completely. How was it they were supposed to live in a shop? Yes, it looked like that shop was all Uncle Halil could find for his dead brother's wife and their three kids left in his care. The rent for his apartment was 50 million, while that of the shop was 20. Other than those who wanted to use it as a warehouse, nobody showed any interest in this alleyway shop. Rather than renting it for 15 million to some textile merchant, the German-Turkish landlord turned the shop into a flat by expanding the toilet and adding a bathroom. He was only concerned about earning another five million.

Their 4-storey apartment building with its vast garden had become a figment of the past. They were now moving their belongings into their new home that was converted from a shop that had huge windows and two rooms when it was partitioned with a curtain. Hatice was also helping out. They were all unhappy and anxious. Her mother asked

Uncle Halil, "How are we going to deal with the winter here?" when she saw the shop's huge pane windows and gaps beneath the steel doors. She assumed they would be able to endure it there until the winter. On the other hand, she heaved an inwardly sigh, as she cried, "How did we end up in this cave?" Her white muslin cloth became drenched as she constantly wiped away her tears.

After painting the windows in lime, hanging the curtains, and positioning the spring mattresses facing each other, the shop somewhat resembled a home. The toilet and bathroom were in together in one place. They weren't accustomed to this, as the toilet was supposed to be outside the house. Now there was a thin wall between the toilet and the corner where they set up the kitchen. The kitchen was a narrow space where all their pots and pans were piled atop of one another. They had a countertop burner without the countertop, a gas tank, and three buckets filled with cracked wheat, lentils and beans. From now on, they were going to wash the dirty dishes in the two square meter space they used as the toilet and bathroom. While Hatice didn't mind this situation very much, her mother and sister were totally devastated. Gulping as they felt ashamed in front of Uncle Halil, they both wanted to cry their hearts out. If only they got back into the truck bed once more and cried until they were hoarse, without feeling ashamed to anyone...

Her sister felt sick to her stomach as she carried the plates and pots into the toilet, as the Dirty Seref who once lived in the back streets came to mind. His complexion was really dark, that's why they call the guy "Dirty Seref." They also called him an atheist as according to the neighborhood, he didn't believe in God. His wife Halime was a woman like everyone else, her 3 sons and 4 daughters were flea-ridden, but they were just like the other kids. Then again, nobody from the neighborhood ever really called on their home because the toilet was inside their home. Of course, that wasn't the problem. There was no toilet door adjacent t the wide space they used as the kitchen. It was for this reason that meals weren't eaten and tea wasn't drunk. Forget about the cleanliness problem, even the neighborhood's most shameless women would be ashamed of having a toilet without a door. They didn't call on Dark Şeref's home unless there was a life-threatening illness. Halime also knew this, and although t she insisted her atheist husband put a door on the toilet, he wouldn't listen to her. Everyone thought Dirty Seref was behaving this way due to his atheism. Word through the grapevine was "The Soviets don't have doors on their toilets and that he was aspiring to be like them." When in fact, Dirty Seref was just too lazy to lift a finger to made the door. He didn't find it in himself to spend the money. On one hand, a doorless toilet served his purpose as guests didn't come around his house. He didn't want to have the neighborhood's gossiping women eating up all the money he made selling fresh produce from his handcart. Let it be known that Dirty Seref, who didn't even participate in Friday prayers and who snuck over to the nearest place to the door to get in a quick prayer in order to avoid their reproachful glances, was an atheist and let them know that the toilet didn't have a door. He was quite at ease with that. On the other hand, Hatice's mother and sister weren't comfortable with the situation at all. For them, condemned to living at the foot of the toilet was sinful and shameful and a big disgrace. They were forced to put up with it.

The toughest experience occurred on the first night. Uncle Halil insisted, "Stay with us tonight." Munise politely declined as she didn't want to take a step into Uncle Halil's home. She couldn't stand Halil's wife Melihat. Melihat's face was as ugly as her heart. She was jealous and stingy. She couldn't even bring herself to welcome them. Had they gone into their home, she would've most certainly stared into their eyes as if counting every bite Munise and her children took. Actually, Munise disliked Melihat from the time when she was young. Melihat was the kind of person who could get the entire neighborhood up in arms over her gossip. She had a soft spot for the neighborhood's young lad, Remzi and her only worry was to deprive lovestruck Munise of this kid with the dark eyebrows. Once, she even defamed Munise in order to achieve this goal, spreading inflammatory gossip throughout the neighborhood to the tune of, "This girl's hot for the market seller Veli." Thank Allah all the girls in the neighborhood knew just how much of a total bullshitter Melihat was. None of them fell for her crap. As it was, Munise loved Remzi starting from the days she became a young lass. Remzi had mutual feelings for her as well. For this reason, he didn't even once turn to look at Melihat, who was too much of an eager beaver to chat with him for five minutes. He saved up his money he earned from working out of town and married Munise. Though Melihat became extremely jealous, she never gave up trying, this time she got her claws into Remzi's docile brother Halil. Halil was such a tame fellow, he was the kind of person who could be tricked by a few kind words. Melihat also had some masterly verbal and expression skills in that she could be quite a vamp sometimes. This was quite opposite of her attitude in general, but she was quite the master on this point. Before the end of the summer when Remzi and Munise got married, she persuaded Halil on the subject of matrimony and married Halil at the end of the summer. She pestered Halil to no end, saying, "Let's move to the big city, and she moved to Istanbul with Halil without waiting for winter to end. While the young girls of the neighborhood along with Munise all felt sorry for Halil, she was quite thrilled to have Melihat out of her hair.

Now, seeing the ugly face of that mean-spirited Melihat, Munise didn't want to listen to her disgusting gossip amidst such a major letdown. She let Hatice go as Halil insisted very much, even though she didn't want her to go. To an extent, she also didn't want Hatice to get too wear and had thought that she would rectify the situation throughout the night with Leyla and Abdurrahman.

Hatice left with her uncle and they boarded a crowded minibus. She was boxed in between some massive guys. The money her uncle had a tough time taking from his pocket was forwarded to the driver. His change was sent back to him via the same hands. The journey didn't last long as it turned out her uncle lived in another part of Esenler. They extricated themselves from the minibus, then passed through a few side streets. They entered a 4-storey building with the name 'Bereket Apartmanı' written over the steel door. The exterior of this building was also ornamented with those small stones. There were bird figures in the corners. Over the apartment, name was a plaque written "In the name of Allah, the compassionate, the merciful" in Arabic script. They went up to the second floor. Uncle Halil opened the door and called out "Melihat." Melihat emerged from behind the door, accompanied by the wafting aroma of cooked food. She frowned the moment she saw Hatice, asking, "Is this Remzi's daughter?" Hatice immediately realized Melihat turned sour when she saw her. So did Uncle Halil… He didn't want to have Hatice sense his wife's grouchiness. He first looked sternly at Melihat, then said to Hatice, "C'mon, let's go into the living room."

All the flats in the neighborhood were the same; painted and plastered on the exterior, with furniture and appliances inside. The bare brick apartments had cushions and caused suffering… Uncle Halil wasn't suffering because of his flat. In fact, there wasn't much standing room in the living room due to all of the furniture. Large facing sofas with red rose designed slipcovers to keep the dirt off of them, and two adjacent la-z-boys covered a major portion of the living room. There was a television set with folded embroidery on top in the right corner. In the other corner was a coffee table with artificial yellow and red flowers. There was also a vivid bird curio fashioned from shiny porcelain. A display case encompassing the entire facing wall. Plates, glasses and dowry items lined up on shelves behind glass covers… There was a distinct decoration in each corner of the living room. While Hatice looked at the red and purple items, Uncle Halil called out, "My girl, where are you?" Hatice knew she had an uncle named Halil and an aunt named Melihat, but she didn't know she had a cousin. Stunned, she wondered if they were the same age? Curious, she began waiting for Uncle Halil's daughter. Her guess was way off the mark. A little girl with a doll in her hand came into the living room. She first looked curiously at the stranger girl sitting in the living room, then she ran over to her father. Uncle Halil said, "Look, my girl, that's your sister Hatice, your uncle's daughter." Hatice liked her cousin with brown hair. Her smiling face wasn't like her mother's.

- What's your name?

- Zahide

- How old are you?

- Seven.

The little girl added laughingly: "I'm going to start school this year." Zahide got off her dad's lap and sat next to Hatice. Uncle Halil turned on the television. The 'Neighborhood Muhktars' was showing on Channel 6. Hatice didn't know any other channel besides TRT 1 and TRT 2. Every day during the week she arrived from school at quarter after five, turned on TRT 1 with her sister and sat on floor cushions. Hatice leaned her head on her sister's shoulder as her sister would caress her long golden hair; They'd watch the love-filled adventures of Sam and Kyle. Hatice's weekend entertainment was 'Sesame Street.' Now she was watching a private station for the first time as the recently opened channels still didn't have any reception in Silvan. While she answered her buck-toothed cousin's questions, she got a kick out of watching her soap opera. She really enjoyed the hilarious situations coffeeman Temel found himself in with his Black Sea dialect. Temel also had a monkey named Teapot. Hatice had become so engrossed in this show, she wasn't even aware that her Uncle Halil had shouted, "Is dinner ready yet?" Her sullen Aunt Melihat snapped back angrily, "It's ready." She brought in a tablecloth with lacy embroidered edges and opened it in the middle of the living room. She then brought in plates and spoons, laid out the metal dining tray and set the table. But she still hadn't welcomed Hatice. She went ballistic when she saw Zahide next to Hatice. In wanting to have her daughter get up from next to Hatice, she yelled, "Stop watching television, get over there and eat your dinner, or I'll kill you."

Just as she was fearful practically every minute of her life, Zahide brought her hands to her belly and hunched over. Zahide thought she was protecting herself when she made this gesture. She was right to do so. While being smacked around by her mother, she felt the least pain when she hunched over and brought her hands to her chest. It was such moments when she hated her mother. Rather than getting a beating, she'd always preferred to be on the streets even if they were dark. She made up her mind, she was going to be on the streets more often than at home when she grows up a little more. Halil sensed his daughter was afraid. He took her by the hand and had her take a seat at the table. Then he called Hatice to the table.

Hatice ate her sullen aunt's food at her uncle's insistence. She didn't even eat the ayran soup she loved very much. She was exhausted and wanted to curl up in a corner and drift off to sleep as soon as possible. Her uncle thought the same way. The moment she got up from the table, he said, "Melihat, open up the couch so the girl can sleep." Melihat looked at the convertible couch and replied, "Why open it up, she's just a tiny little girl." She took the spite she had for Munise out on Hatice by not opening out the couch. Though she was considerate enough to bring a pillow and comforter from the adjacent room, she didn't spread out a bedsheet on the couch out of utter laziness and sheer evil that swelled in her heart. Had it been any other time, Hatice wouldn't have slept a wink as she mulled over Melihat's bigotry. But she was so tired that she crashed the instant she stretched out on the couch her aunt couldn't bother to turn into a bed. She couldn't even cover herself properly with the comforter.

With the exception of Munise and Leyla, practically all of Istanbul slept soundly that night. Especially Abdurrahman, who fell asleep the moment he laid his head on his pillow.

Munise and Leyla still had more tears to shed before they went to sleep. They were making a commendable effort to turn the musty-smelling shop into a livable home. Pausing what they were doing to perform their evening prayers. Their hearts were crushed even further as they cried sentimentally when they prostrated themselves.

They resumed their chores after the nighttime prayers. Abdurrahman was sleeping like a log on the floor mattress. After thoroughly cleaning and wiping down the place, they removed all their belonging from burlap sacks and chests and stacked them next to the walls. They finally were able to turn the huge shop like space into an atmosphere resembling a home. They laid the clean carpets the civilian police would no longer be treading with their shoes over the concrete floor. They lined cushions in the corners and closed off the humungous shop windows with bright curtains. They positioned the wardrobe, which got nicked and scratched in the move, next to the TV stand… However, they didn't feel fully settled in without placing the Quran in its place. Munise wouldn't have felt at ease any other way. Actually, the moment she learned the direction of Mecca from Uncle Halil in the morning, she called Abdurrahman over by her side. She wanted him to drive a nail into the wall facing Mecca. Though he didn't understand her motive, Abdurrahman was able to drive the nail into the wall only after hitting his hand a few times. Now it was time… She took the Quran from its hand-embroidered slipcover on the tray. Caressing the embroidered cover for awhile, she broke down and started crying. Leyla embroidered that cover in the shade of the trees enveloping the gardens in Silvan like a fence. There were two intertwining Arabic 'waw' letters on top of the cover. They represented The Almighty. In the Quran, the 'waw' was six in the calculation system, depending on the letters. '66' was the equivalent to the word 'Allah' in Sufism. Leyla wouldn't pick up the needle and thread to embroider the 'waw's without doing her ablutions first. She heard about the meaning of the 'waw' from her grandfather Hacı Ali Osman.

The 'waw' was the six conditions of being faithful and was the tale of the creation of the universe. It became an embryo that found life in the mother's womb once spirit was blown, it prostrated to Allah and became a follower who submitted humbly once it achieved perfection.

Worried about setting up their new home, mother and daughter performed their evening prayers at an unprecedented late hour of the night. She was ritually clean. She didn't want to sleep with the fear that she'd miss her morning prayers. Before she hung her Quran on the wall, she wanted to read some relaxing verses from the Quran while waiting for the call to prayer. She removed the Quran, an heirloom from her father Hacı Ali Osman, from its cover. Munise read it well and knew the Quranic reading style. She was taught by her hadji father, He was a farmer, but not the run-of-the-mill sort. He took lessons from a sheikh in Bitlis and was a saintly man who was educated in a madrasah. Munise opened to the 'Tekvir' sura. The 'Tekvir' was one of the suras she learned the meaning of from her father. She got goosebumps every time she read this sura. It was as if each letter was refreshing her belief. The blood in her veins retreated whenever she began reading the verses "When the sun halts in its path, the stars become fuzzy and go out, and the mountains move." The sura ended with the verse, "You can't wish for anything as long as the Creator of Universe, Allah doesn't wish for anything. She fully believed in this. First, she wiped her tears with a white muslin cloth, then glanced over at her kids sleeping on the floor mattress. It was a night she longed for her Hatice. She submitted to her fate. Her hand with its old age blemishes caressed the Quran's glue-scented page, as she began reading. It wasn't long before the call to prayer spread throughout the neighborhood. Munise finished the verse she was reading then woke up Leyla. Though she poked Abdurrahman, she didn't manage to get him to his feet. An exhausted mother and daughter performed their morning prayers, then went immediately back to sleep. Two hours hadn't passed when Leyla was awoken by someone tapping on the window. She was scared and woke up her mother. They were expecting Uncle Halil and Hatice, but not this early. Leyla froze in her tracks when she opened the steel door, its window painted over with lime. Standing behind her, Munise was also dumbfounded. Leyla gulped and could only say, "It's Yılmaz." Yılmaz… Yılmaz wanted by the organization, Yılmaz, who was the reason Munise's squeaky clean carpets were desecrated with filthy boots and shoes practically once a week, the Yılmaz who cause them to migrate to the big city… He was there now, facing them. Where did he come from, how did he know they settled there? Most importantly, where was he when their home was turned upside-down by those carrying state identities for the past year?

After getting over their initial shock, they showed Yılmaz in. Actually, they weren't too keen on showing him in as they were still afraid of the organization and being raided. But there was nothing to do as it was a relative of theirs at the door...

Yılmaz had been in Istanbul for a long time. Thinking he'd show off to those around him and make some money in the process, he fled to the big city a long time ago due to his shady relations that affiliated him with the organization in Silvan. His fear of getting caught drove him to get himself a phony national I.D. card with the name 'Ekrem Tasli' and had been working in a garment sweatshop. This was a temporary job as he had plans to find an illegal way to get to Germany. He was living and going between home, work and the tavern without sticking out like a sore thumb. When he got off work, sometimes he'd hang out in a park that had nothing but a rusty old swing with busted chains. The park was a hangout not so much for little kids, but rather for a bunch of likely lads who spent the money remaining from the weekly cash they handed over to their dads every Saturday night on Maltepe cigarettes. The poor boys working in the sweatshops liked smoking filtered Maltepes. Lads who were broke generally smoked filterless Birincis. Youngbloods climbing up the wretched social ladder would light up Maltepes, squat down and plunge into a heavy conversation. Yılmaz enjoyed chatting with these young kids, who were as poor and heroic as Yılmaz Güney in his films, as revolutionary and rebellious as Ahmet Kaya in his songs, and as arabesque and passionate as Ibrahim Tatlıses in his folk songs. He'd spend his time until the sun went down with his little friends who were younger than himself in that park, its non-green soil turned into concrete where soccer matches were held in daily clothes and goalposts were marked with rocks. Yılmaz enjoyed chatting with Eyüp the most. Eyüp was 15 years old and at odds with life. He didn't like the neighborhood he lived in, the school he was enrolled in, nor his mother or father who bore him. It got to the point where he no longer even enjoyed toking on Maltepes with his neighborhood buddies. His mind was elsewhere. He frequently held one-on-one conversations with Yılmaz. The stories of the organization, most of which were blown out of proportion, he heard from Yılmaz, who always had a pack of Marlboro longs in his shirt pocket while perched atop a bench with a handful of boards missing, never failed to get his blood boiling. One day, after the school-year ended, he whispered into Yılmaz's ear.

- I want to go into the mountains too.

- What mountains, dude?

Yılmaz, who was planning to make a getaway to Germany, didn't want wind up in any trouble. He tried to maintain his distance from Eyüp, but he couldn't save his ass. He finally gave up. He swore for the umpteenth time, "For fuck's sake, how the fuck did I ever get involved with this punk?" Then again, he caved into Eyüp's demand, thinking he'd run off at the mouth and get him in even bigger trouble than he was already in. He set up all the connections in two months. First Eyüp was going to travel to Van, and then over to Hakkari. From there, he'd end up in the camp. They booked his ticket to Van for Thursday at six in the morning.

Eyüp's family was from Diyarbakır. After repeating his third grade twice, he barely got out of junior-high school. He had two elder brothers, one of whom was an imam waiting to fill a vacant position in Malatya, while the other was a janitor with the State Water Utility. His father Mahmut earned his livelihood selling chicken and rice from a cart. While Eyüp had no desire to become an imam or a janitor, he never for a single moment considered selling rice-on-the-run like his father. However, he also had no idea what he wanted to be. The only thing he knew was to get the hell out of there.

Riceman Mahmut suspected his youngest son Eyüp was ducking out of sight lately. Some days, he'd head back home without selling all his rice and watch his son who'd meet up with his friends in the park from afar. Lately, he'd seen a tall guy with a dark complexion always wearing a white shirt and black pants, his black hair growing from behind, next to his son. Once again, they were talking in hushed tones, perched up on the park bench. Riceman Mahmut roosted in a corner next to the butcher, eyeing the park from a safe distance. Their conversation went into overtime this time as it was ten at night. They finally split up as Eyüp appeared pensive. He was walking with his head out in front, without looking anywhere. In fact, he was so lost in thought that he wouldn't have even noticed his father waiting in the corner just ahead had he passed by his side. Riceman Mahmut smelled a rat. What exactly was going on? Did they do something evil to his child? Or maybe they wanted his kid to do something evil? Which one? Both possibilities were horrendous. He slipped in behind his son who passed within a couple of meters from him. Following him at a safe distance all the way to their flat, he constantly muttered prayers under his breath. Riceman Mahmut was a 'hafiz.' While pleading to Allah for his son, he had murmured practically the entire Quran. However, he was still perturbed. He entered the flat after his son. Eyüp had long since stretched out on the sofa. Riceman Mahmut didn't want to interrogate his son. He said, "It'll wait until morning." His wife Nazmiye brewed some smuggled tea, but he didn't drink it. He conducted his night prayers and went to bed, but he couldn't sleep. Tossing and turning in bed, he explained the situation to Nazmiye. Now both of them were writhing about in bed, all the way until the morning call to prayer was heard. In getting up to pray, Nazmiye exited the bedroom to conduct her ablutions. Just then, she heard the sound of the front door. Half-asleep, she looked anxiously in the living room. Her son wasn't on the sofa. Where could Eyüp have gone at this time of the morning? She ran immediately over to the front door, then stepped outside in her flannel nightgown. Meanwhile, she was trying to tuck her white hair under her headscarf. She spotted Eyüp as he turned the corner at the end of the street. She shouted from behind, "Where are you going, son!?" Upon hearing his mother's voice, Eyüp didn't bother looking back as he picked up the pace. He knew he'd never be able to go again if he stopped. Nazmiye caught up to him in her barefeet and grabbed her son's arm. She was gasping for breath.

- Where are you going, son?

- I'm going to the mountains and from there, I'm going to Germany. Leave my arm alone, I've got a bus to catch.

He started running, the moment he broke free of his mother's grasp. Nazmiye collapsed in the middle of the street. She wept aloud then pulled herself together in order to tell her husband. She ran home and shrieked like banshees. She jabbed fists into her husband, who was snoring with his mouth wide open. "Get up, man, get up, Eyüp's gone, get up." Riceman Mahmut woke up in fear. "Where'd he go, whadya saying, woman?" Riceman Mahmut, who had just been sleeping so soundly that a battalion of charging tanks wouldn't have disturbed him in the least, was now bright eyed and bushy-tailed. Slipping his trousers over his pyjamas and tossing a shirt over his back, he went charging out of the flat. He incessantly pressed the doorbell of his neighbor, the stallholder Davut. Davut had a van and sold cotton skirts and blouses in bazaars around town. Davut's eyes were swollen as he opened his front door. He asked, "What happened, neighbor?" when he saw Riceman Mahmut bawling his eyes out. Riceman Mahmut blurted out pleadingly, "Davut, we've got to get to Topkapı right now, my son's run away from home!" He couldn't tell Davut that his son intended on joining the organization. As a Bulgarian immigrant, Davut had no understanding of such situations. Davut immediately ran back inside and grabbed his keys to the van. Without any time to put on a change of clothing, he said to Riceman Mahmut, "C'mon neighbor, let's move!" On the way, Stallholder Davut asked Riceman Mahmut, "Any idea what bus Eyüp's going to board at the station?" He was stunned when a blubbering Riceman Mahmut replied, "I don't know." As he wondered how they were supposed to find Eyüp at the enormous station, Riceman Mahmut blurted out, "We can check the bus companies counters that operate out toward our way." Riceman Mahmut knew those who joined the organization generally passed over the border from either Hakkâri or Siirt. The first places they had to check were the counters of these cities. Stallholder Davut was driving his yellow Ford Transit van like a bat out of hell. The skirts and blouses he carried in the back were flying all over the place, They wanted to get to the station before Eyüp. They arrived there at five and started looking for Eyüp. One by one, they searched the buses heading in the direction of Hakkari, Siirt, and Van. They checked all the counters but didn't find Eyüp. Stallholder Davut shouted, "What are we gonna do, shall we call the cops?" Riceman Mahmut suddenly recoiled when he heard the word 'police.' The police needn't get involved in this business. He was afraid as he couldn't throw his son in jail while he was trying to save him. He said, "Let's wait a bit." They learned the departure times of all the buses from their counters. While a bus was leaving for Hakkari at five-thirty, another was scheduled to leave for Van at six. They also learned there was another one heading for Van at two in the afternoon. According to Riceman Mahmut's guess, Eyüp was going to board either the five-thirty or six o'clock bus.

They began waiting within visual range of both the Van and Hakkâri counters. It was 05:30 and Eyüp was still nowhere in sight. Riceman Mahmut's face grew haggard with anguish as he began to lose his temper. Five or six minutes hadn't gone by when his eyes suddenly sparkled. He spotted his son at a distance and he wasn't alone. He had that guy next to him again. Riceman Mahmut leapt from where he stood without saying anything to Davut. His anguish had turned into a fiery ball of nerves as he started running towards Yılmaz. Davut was also behind him… Eyüp froze like a deer caught in a car's headlights when he saw his father. Yılmaz turned around and started running away. But Riceman Mahmut grabbed Yılmaz's long hair drooping from his neck. He pulled Yılmaz backwards, then clutched his throat. He squeezed him so hard that Yılmaz couldn't breathe. His face turned bright red as he was forced to sit on the ground. While Stallholder Davut was on one side, his son Eyüp was trying to rescue Yılmaz from Riceman Mahmut's grasp. Eyüp was begging his father, "Leave him alone father." However, Riceman Mahmut had no intention of letting Yılmaz go after following him for so long with such hatred. He screamed at the top of his lungs.

- I'm gonna kill this son of a bitch.

- Wait a minute, Godammit, Mahmut. You don't wanna get us in trouble.

- Dad, stop it, dad! Don't do it, I swear to God, Daddddd!

Riceman Mahmut had totally lost his self-control to the point of removing his pocket knife he carried in his belt for sunnah and pressed it up to Yılmaz's throat. He didn't want to go against Allah's command to 'not kill' and become a murderer. But he also wanted to punish this guy who deliberately wanted to send his son to his death. The clerks in the ticket offices, the bus drivers with their thick moustaches, their helpers waiting for their departure times with their ties tied stiffly around their collars, as well as curious passengers standing about all gathered around the scene of the crime. Some of them intervened to break it up. Once some of them shouted, "Call the police," Riceman Mahmut came to his senses. The police were never to get involved in this business. After yelling, "If I ever see you again in the neighbor I'll cut you to shreds," he let go of Yılmaz's collar. In letting go, he also slammed his fist onto Yılmaz's nose. Tongue-tied out of fear, Yılmaz didn't even realize the warmth of the blood pouring from his nose because the coldness of the knife was still on his throat. He got to his feet and began running for his life. His heels struck his butt. He even flung off his black jacket and threw it on the ground so as to lighten his load. Blood was discharging from his nose in copiously, turning his white shirt crimson red.

Yılmaz didn't go to work after this incident and didn't want to be seen in the neighborhood. He stopped dropping by the coffeehouse and park as well. He ran to the organization the night he was freed from Riceman Mahmut's sharp pocket knife and told them, "Speed up my German affair." He locked himself away in his flat waiting for news. He didn't emerge from his home in the morning but only when he was really bored did he venture outside once darkness enveloped. Once outside, he didn't spend any time in the neighborhood, preferring to catch his breath in the nightclubs and taverns in Aksaray. Some days, he stopped to see Uncle Halil before heading into the nightclub scene. His uncle knew he worked in a leather shop in Laleli. Rather than the retail leather business, and customers they talked more about his bandaged nose, and the surgery he had on it during his last visit with Uncle Halil. He told his uncle he had the cartilage removed from his nose because he couldn't breathe. Their conversation meandered as they talked about their hometown. Yılmaz asked Uncle Halil, "How are my aunt and her family?" He had wondered for a long time. He was overcome with excitement once he learned his aunt and cousins moved to Istanbul. Leyla dropped into his mind. He really ran after Leyla back home and would've married her had he not joined the organization. His aunt most likely wouldn't have approved, but he still would've eloped and married her. He wanted to see Leyla and wasted no time getting her address from Uncle Halil. He quickly downed a glass of smuggled tea, burning his mouth and tongue in the process. He went out of his uncle's flat, saying, "I'm leaving,

I've got to be at work early in the morning." He wanted to go to Leyla straight away. He looked at his watch, which he kept in his pocket instead of on his wrist as it reminded him of handcuffs. It was getting late. He thought about going home, but decided that wasn't the greatest idea. "Leyla's in İstanbul, so why would I go home?" He flagged down a cab and headed to Aksaray instead. He was a regular in one of the basement taverns in Aksaray. It was a murky venue where upper middle-aged women sang folk songs out of tune in revealing dresses on a tiny stage. There were smoky red and purple backlights, barely illuminating the sins, covert lovers, twisted playboys and regrets without any point of return.

Women meandered from table to table wearing slit dresses making it easy for customers to slip a hand between their legs, ordering whiskey and wine for customers who were worthless save for their soon-to-be emptied wallets from bills swollen beyond belief. Knowing full well he was going to be ripped off, Yılmaz was also a customer who enjoyed spending time with these heavily made-up women. After having dropped by there on several occasions, he was considered a regular by the waiters and hostesses. The moment he entered the door, a frail waiter walked towards Yılmaz, saying, "Welcome, sir," treating him like a special customer as he led him over to one of the tables in front. He was so frail, nobody would've noticed him if it hadn't been for his synthetic white shirt that sparkled in the dim light. This waiter knew well what Yılmaz wanted. He began lining up appetizers on the table without waiting to be asked. He also brought a 70 ml. bottle of arrack with a single glass. Yılmaz drank his arrack without water. But this time, he said "No thanks." The last thing he wanted to do was drink arrack and confront Leyla in a drunken state. The waiter was stunned as he knew quite well Yılmaz was an imbiber. Straightening his hair he stuck to his head with brilliantine, the waiter said, "Fine sir, so what will it be then?" Yılmaz asked for a cola. The frail waiter pulled his baggy trousers upwards. He didn't have it in him to ask, "Dumbass, why'd you show up without any money?" He grinned and settled for muttering this question on the tip of his tongue as he turned around and went off.

Yılmaz was impatient. He didn't even hear the tunes sung by the crooner on stage at the top of her lungs. If was any other time, he'd keep the beat and accompany the folk tune. In fact, he had gone on stage in an inebriated state and grabbed the mic on more than one occasion. While he couldn't keep track of how many glasses of arrack he drank during previous outings, this time around he had no idea how many colas he downed. The two hours since he entered the joint seemed like two days. It was two at night and he gazed his eyes around him. There were two guys whispering in each other's ears at the table to his right. Especially in all this racket… The next table over featured four or five teenagers who clearly looked like they came with their monthly pocket money savings or wages. Sitting next to them were women old enough to be their mothers. It was obvious they were going to be urged to willingly leave all their money in their pockets on the table after two kisses and two glasses. Meanwhile, those who managed to caress a leg and touch a breast would have tales to tell for months ahead. For sure, it would take months for them to save money in order to be able to return to the bottomless pit of a venue where they were swindled. Turning his back, Yılmaz gazed at a group that was as crowded as a wedding party. Tables full of fruit platters and snacks were brought together. Sitting around them was an elderly man wearing a jacket as large as a shepherd's gaberdine, along with four middle-aged punks looking like a bunch of greasers in black suits... Next to them were the youngest girls tavern womanizers would ever see. There was one in particular, her face was as fresh as a daisy. Her face was shiny even in that darkness. It was crystal clear she couldn't have been more than 15… Yılmaz's eyes latched onto that girl. He took pity on her. There weren't many such cases in which Yılmaz would actually give a fuck about. But this time, he didn't know if he was influenced by Leyla or what, but he really pitied the girl. He said inwardly, "What a shame, what's she doing in such a dump at her age?" as he gave up looking at her left side. He turned in front of him and took a sip from his cola like he was drinking arrack. He had just taken a second sip when a voice rose from behind him, "What the fuck are you staring at, bitch?" He didn't have a chance to turn around when a fist struck his neck, making him spray the cola in his mouth all over the table. Nobody heard the sound of the glass shattering on the floor due to the raucous music that spread from the stage throughout the tavern. Had he not loosened his hand, he was going to slam to the table along with the glass. He could've swallowed that huge glass. He qucikly drew his hand to his waist. That knife Riceman Mahmut had pressed against his throat had frightened him so much that he started carrying the weapon he had hidden in the stove hole for a long time. As he drew his gun, he got up and turned around. He was facing one of the punks wearing a black suit. He understood the small girl was to be his victim tonight. He stuck his gun in the punk's eye. Yelling, "I'll stick your hand up your ass, motherfucker," he held the horseshoe-sized buckle of his belt and pulled it towards the punk. Suddenly, the waiters, the tavern owners sitting in their office, their friends, the indispensable tough guys of arguments all gathered at the scene of the crime. These same tough guys who didn't make a sound while sweet 15-year old girls were pimped in corners of the tavern and raped until the morning light had taken up the negotiating role of making sure those involved in this armed conflict return to a sense of calm without anyone getting hurt. They were all as sensible as rescuing hostages. They didn't want Yılmaz to do anything he would regret later on. Now the police were going to arrive, accompanied by the district attorney, the press was going to descend on the place … If he's going to shoot, let him do his shooting outside. Yılmaz thought that was all a bunch of bullshit.

Goddamnit, had you been real men, you screwballs wouldn't have gone up against each other to be the first to have a go at that kid, but his wits got the best of him. These words weren't good for anything but a reason for them to gang together and kick the living shit out of him.

The punk's color paled as his left eye looked down at the elderly man sitting at the table pleaded with Yılmaz, "Son, I think there's been a misunderstanding, we're sorry." Yılmaz was not distracted by the old man's words, but rather by the single solitary tooth dangling from the upper palate of his mouth. When in fact his lower teeth were shining like perfect pearls. Everyone was saying something else as they all tried to calm Yılmaz down. Actually, Yılmaz didn't need any of them to calm down that night. In recalling Leyla, he regretted drawing his weapon. He shouted, "Mother fucker, pray …" but didn't go any further. He wanted to say, "Mother fucker, pray I've got Leyla now," but couldn't say this either. He didn't want Leyla's name to be remembered in this filthy place. He lowered his weapon, and had to pull his hand back when the punk said, "Let me kiss you, man!" He looked at his watch. It was two at night. He got to his feet and asked for his bill. As he had cola instead of arrack that night, he absorbed the lesser rip-off and stepped outside. The single-toothed man bid him farewell at the door of the tavern. The instant he freed himself from the old prick, he decided to go home and put on a change of clothes. Then he was going to stop by his barber and have his hair combed out. He didn't have enough patience to get on a minibus that operated at night. In reality, he was scared shitless of running into Riceman Mahmut. He flagged down the first taxi he saw.

- Let's head for Esenler, bro.

He still had that 15-year old girl on his mind. He felt disturbed about the whole situation. A tough battle was being fought in his head between his conscious and logic. How did he leave that child in the midst of those assholes knowing full well what would happen to her? His conscious was swinging a sword at logic with this question. Going in defensive mode, his logic did everything necessary out of fear and threats in order not to relinquish dominance with its shield, "They're gonna kill you, dude."

- Hey, bro, turn in here!

- What happened, did you forget something?

His conscious emerged victorious. "Dude, how many lives have you taken up to now, so why not save a life before you die and kick the bucket." Having added the yeast of ruthlessness to his soul, logic bit the dust; it succumbed to compassion, which dropped into his heart on occasion. The cabbie turned the wheel before Yılmaz had to say it again and swerved at the Aksaray turn off. The meter was running regardless of how far he drove... Then again, his curiosity got the better of him as he looked in his rearview mirror. Noticing his curious looks in the mirror, Yılmaz could only manage to say "child."... As they hadn't gotten very far, they dropped into Aksaray in less than 10 minutes. Yılmaz got out of the taxi on the avenue behind the tavern. Fine, he was going to save the kid, but after the latest incident, he knew for a fact that the bodyguards at the door weren't going to let him back into the joint, at least not tonight. He also didn't want to do anything stupid that would put his life in jeopardy. While saving a life, he didn't want to lose his own without seeing Leyla. He walked down the avenue a bit and peered about once he got in front of the ruins of an historical fountain. Muttering, "Where the fuck is that faggot?", he took a few steps towards the back of the fountain ruins. He wasn't mistaken. Pimp Ferhat was pimping a Russian broad to a construction worker who was ready to pony up his entire weekly wages. Yılmaz was familiar with these types from the nights he hung out with Pimp Ferhat. Those who just got paid their weekly stipend would head straight for Aksaray. They all had traces of wall plaster from their construction jobs on their faces. He blew off the negotiating worker and confronted Pimp Ferhat. "Finish up your business, we've gotta talk." They glanced at each other in affirmation. He then headed back to the avenue and light up a smoke. Inhaling deeply, he exhaled the smoke into the air as Leyla floated into his mind. He was distracted by a boy on the opposite sidewalk. He held had a photograph, as he continuously fell into the arms of passersby. The assets of the club he worked for were in that photo. He'd start off saying, "Hey, lookin' for a fun time?" and got a kickback if he was able to hustle guys into the club who were turned on by his "hooters and ass" spiel. After gaping at the guy who stuck his left hand in his pocket to play with his dick while ogling a group photograph of hostesses wearing slitted skirts, Yılmaz chuckled involuntarily. "Go ahead, scratch all you want buddy, they're going to sock you with such a bill, you won't know what hit you…"

After gaping at the guy who stuck his left hand in his pocket to play with his dick while ogling a group photograph of hostesses wearing slitted skirts, Yılmaz chuckled involuntarily.

Pimp Ferhat emerged from behind the fountain rubble without giving Yılmaz the chance to get wound up about Leyla. "What the fuck, was he a laborer or what?" Pimp Ferhat faced this question without opening his mouth. He said indifferently, "Yeah, sure, what's up?" As someone pimping to broke-dick womanizers, it wasn't surprising his customer he was panning off elderly gold-toothed broads from practically unknown lands in the Caucasus as Russian was a construction worker. "Nothing, forgetaboutit" said Yılmaz… "Fuck it, we've got work to do!"

Grabbing Pimp Ferhat by the arm, he thrust him once again behind the fountain ruins.

- You're going to go to my hangout. They've got a new girl working there. I don't care how you do it, but you get her out of there and bring her to me.

- Man, they've give you the girl at the place had you said anything. You think they'd keep you from that whore?

- Bugger off, dumbass, why would I ask for the girl I'm going to fuck from you? This is something else.

- WTF, if you're not going to bang her, whadya want to do, get engaged?

- Don't fuck with me, asshole, listen to me. I'm not going to leave that fresh as a daisy girl in the hands of those pimps. I picked a fight that's why I can't go in there now. You can find a way.

- Man, how can I get that girl outside, they'd riddle me with holes.

- Nothing's going to happen to you. You know very well how to get in and outta there. Bring me that girl and you can spit in my face if I don't take care of your Germany business.

Pimp Ferhat's eyeballs leapt out of their sockets when he heard the word 'Germany.' Ever since his childhood, he had been saving his kurush just so he could go to Germany. He was aching to travel even if it meant illegally. In fact, once he risked the trip for this dream by squeezing into the corner of the back of a big rig loaded with steel rods. However, he along with seven other poor souls were caught before they reached Tekirdağ, and his 5,000 Deutschmarks he had paid human smugglers were gone with the wind. But he trusted Yılmaz. Besides, he owed him a debt of gratitude. With Yılmaz' assistance, he was able to wrestle himself out of the grasp of two adolescent pimps who wanted to take over his avenue. Had that huge switchblade of his rival pimp plunged into his thigh, his new nickname would've become 'The Lame Pimp.' With the sensibility of the neighborhood mukhtar who received an order from a higher authority to "follow everything that goes on and report to us," he understood right away which girl Yılmaz was referring to as he followed who was going in and out of the clubs in the area. Going into the club was easy but how was he going to call the girl over, how was he going to convince her and most importantly, how was he going to get her outside? He thought about this from the time he turned onto the avenue until he entered the street where the tavern was located. He made his plan. It wasn't necessary to enter through the front door and draw everyone's attention. He was going to go around the building and jump over the garden wall and enter the club through the dishwashing station door. All the cooks and waiters knew him, as he'd come and gone the same way while fleeing the police. It'll be just right if he went inside panting for air as though he was running from the cops again. He did just as he planned. As he dived inside, he saw two kids with dark complexions whose names he couldn't remember doing the washing up. He greeted them, then walked towards the door of the scullery. He poked his eye inside and peered into the secluded corners of the joint. He saw the girl Yılmaz mentioned. She was stuck in the middle of the guys around her like a kitten. His entry plan went as planned, he saw the girl too, now what? He turned around and spotted a chair at the edge of the table where the dirty dishes were stacked high. He watched the dishwasher kids for a while. One would scrub the dirty plate with the sponge in his hand, then stick it in the basin of soapy water and remove it while the other rinsed it off. There was a rhythmic order accompanied by the 'shak shak' noise made by the porcelain plates being stacked on atop the other. Just then, a pipsqueak waiter came into the scullery with a cigarette he was about to light up.. Pimp Ferhat didn't remember the name of the pipsqueak waiter but he knew damn well he was a shifty character who'd even sell his mother down the river for money. The pipsqueak waiter lit his cigarette and said slickly to Pimp Ferhat, "Welcome, bro, whadya doin' here, hey come inside." Pimp Ferhat leapt from where he was standing. He called out to the pipsqueak waiter, "Lemme get a smoke from you." In taking the smoke, he said, "Let's fire them up in this fresh air," motioning to the garden out back. It was his intention to get the pipsqueak waiter away from the dishwashers. As they stepped into the garden, he stuck 20 million into the pipsqueak waiter's pocket. "Hey man, I want you to call the new girl inside out here." Glancing at the money in his pocket from the corner of his eye, Pimp Ferhat stuck another 20 million in the pipsqueak waiter's pocket before he could say, "Bro, they'll burn me." "Don't drag on about it, we're going to talk for a few minutes, that's all." He sort of understood the reason of Pimp Ferhat's generosity. He knew Pimp Ferhat, who normally wouldn't give up a single kurush even with a blade thrust against his throat, was a good friend of Yılmaz, the hell-raiser of the night. If Pimp dropped into the tavern through the back door, then he was definitely up to something. Then again, the pipsqueak waiter didn't push Pimp Ferhat very far as he didn't want to jeopardize the money in his pocket. He said, "Okay," and went inside. He said, "They're calling her from the office for five minutes" and led the girl away from the table. He convinced the wolves next to him, saying, "She'll be right back, there's an important matter that needs to be taken care of." He whispered "Follow me" into the girl's ear as she trudged towards the management office as though she was going to her death. It wasn't long before they found themselves in the scullery garden. Pimp Ferhat said, "Just give us a few moments" and sent the pipsqueak waiter back inside.

- Can you go up that wall?

- What Wall? Why?

- Don't ask why, can you go up it?

- I can't go up it.

- I'll help you.

- Why?

- Whadya mean why? Don't you want to be rescued from here?

- Who wouldn't want to be rescued from death?

The poor girl said 'yeah' to Pimp Ferhat's offer without knowing who wants to save her. Perhaps she was going to find herself in even bigger trouble. But even the word 'rescue' sounded nice enough on its own. She took off her high heels and tossed them into the garden so she could walk more comfortably.

Pimp Ferhat picked up the girl and lifted her towards the top of the wall. Then he followed her over the garden wall. They wandered through the garden of the adjacent apartment and went out onto the street without passing in front of the club. Wandering around the lower side of the street, they came out on the back avenue. They found Yılmaz behind the fountain.

- What's your name?

- Ceyda.

- Forget that, what's the name your mother gave you?

- Leyla.

Leyla… Yılmaz felt a pang of sorrow in his heart. "I'm glad I came." All his reluctance he had from his standoff earlier that night dissipated in the air together with the smoke of his cigarette.

- How old are you, Leyla?

- 15, bro.

- 15?

- Yes bro.

- How did you ever end up in these parts? Where are your folks?

- I ran away from an orphanage, bro.

- Why'd you run away girl, what was your problem?

- There was a young guy who fixed the electrical stuff at the orphanage, bro. He said, I've got a shop, I'll look after you. We were going to get married and he was going to rescue me from the orphanage. I was going to have a home. I loved him, bro... He sold me to these guys the night I ran away.

Leyla couldn't hold back much longer as she started crying. Yılmaz didn't ask "Did they do anything bad to you?" He didn't want to open up the wounds of a child dandied up like a woman and toss her tiny body down bloody crimson wells. He only asked her hometown and wanted to know where her orphanage was located. It wasn't in another city, and in fact was only a few districts from where they were. Well, was the child who was supposed to be in bed at the orphanage at that hour going to sleep in the bed of toothless old shitbags? Yılmaz couldn't come to terms with this.

- C'mon, we're outta here.

- Where we going, bro?

- Back where you came from.

- How can I go there like this, bro?

Yılmaz looked again at Ceyda. No, at Leyla. Right, how was she supposed to go back to the orphanage dressed like a hostess wearing such heavy makeup? He looked at Pimp Ferhat. They reached a visual understanding once again.

Pimp Ferhat said, "I'll be right back," and returned 15 minutes later. He brought back dresses of the women he panned off as Russian to the laborers. He also had a pair of slippers in his hand. "Let's go to the front side now, nobody will see you there as you change your clothes."

It wasn't long before Leyla emerged in front of the fountain rubble in a skirt that was temporarily tied around her waist and a blouse that stretched down to her knees. Meanwhile, Yılmaz washed her face with a liter bottle of water he bought from an off-license shop and dried her off with the end of the dress she discarded. The heavy makeup hadn't been entirely wiped off, but at least the whore signage on her forehead had been removed by its nails and tossed to the ground. She regained her childhood as they got in a taxi together with Yılmaz. Yılmaz told the cabbie where the orphanage was as they drove off. As the taxi proceeded on down the road, Yılmaz grinned at Pimp Ferhat as he said, "Disappear for a while, I'll find you, Hans." He took a deep breath and leaned backwards. There was Ferdi Tayfur's incomparable melodies coming from the cassette deck and calmness in his heart… From the rearview mirror, he looked at Leyla sitting in the back seat for a long time. He felt sorry for her condition. Goddamn, the justice in this world. I'll fuck you and the horse you rode in on…

Leyla didn't get out of the cab in front of the orphanage, so Yılmaz called out to her sadly, 'Go on, get a move on,' as if it was his own sister who was leaving him. He poked his head out the cab's front window and reached out with his right hand to stick some money into Leyla's left hand. He admonished her, "I don't know if you want to study at school or find yourself a decent job, but whatever you do from now on, just trust yourself, got it?" He gave Leyla a word of advice as he got back in the cab. After seeing Leyla pass through the orphanage door, he said to the cabbie, "Okay, it's time to take me home…"

It had become quite light outside when he arrived at his home. He didn't want to sleep in order not to wander about like a drunk. He took a shower. After drying his hair, he sat on his bed and pondered what to wear. In the meanwhile, he realized all his shirts were the same color. He didn't have any striped or checkered shirts. He tried on and took off all the shirts in his cabinet. Finally, he decided to wear a black shirt. A black shirt to go with a black outfit… Freshly dyed pig-nosed leather-soled shoes...

Fearful of someone stepping on his feet or his clothes getting dirty on a minibus or city bus, he hailed down another cab. He wanted to face Leyla like he was going up on stage. He was on the stage of the lime-smelling house within a half-hour. Sitting in the puffiest of cushions lined up in the corner, he was perched right next to Abdurrahman, who from the look of the purple blotches under his eyes, looked like he hadn't quite caught up on his sleep. Munise and Leyla were still at a loss for words. They'd spread a carpet out in the middle of the concrete space of the shop they turned into a home. They sat in the exact center of that carpet and stared at Yılmaz' mouth. There weren't concerned in the least about the outfit he thought about for two hours in the morning of his blood and thunder night. When in fact, Yılmaz was sure his outfit caught their attention. He thought there wasn't a soul on Earth who wouldn't like the black shirt with its yellow embroidered collar he wore as part of his black pants and jacket. His mind was on the stressful night he had and was thankful he was able to confront Leyla safe and sound. But as the hours advanced, he collapsed into the trepidation of "what the hell have I gotten myself into?"

While Yılmaz calculated the shit he was going to find himself in while abducting the girl from the nightclub, he couldn't bear Munise. "Son, you put us through a lot of trouble," as she started weeping.

- Auntie, I beg you, please don't cry.

- I left my home and neighborhood and ended up in this cave. This is worse than I could possibly have imagined, son.

In getting Kurdish responses to his Turkish sentences, Yılmaz had one eye on Leyla. Her tears were also running down her cheeks. They went quiet for a while. This silence only served to rachet up Yılmaz's fears carried over from last night. The silence that descended upon the lime-smelling hole-in-the-wall was suddenly pierced by the racket of a pit saw coming from the carpentry shop next door. Someone began shouting …

- Hey kid, you're cocking the whole thing up, either do the lacquering right or don't do it at all!

They were all stunned. All except Yılmaz... As though the sound of a saw wasn't enough so early in the morning, some lout was ranting and raving. Master Rafik was operating the pit saw. He got the window and door business at a construction site two streets over and started cutting the wooden window frames early in the morning. He assigned his journeyman the task of lacquering the sandpapered particle board doors. Having taken the doors out into the street, the journeyman also carried out iron pedestals resembling goalposts. He laid the doors on top of the pedestals and was applying lacquer on them one by one with a spray gun. Due to the journeyman's indexterity, the pressurized lacquer fell over a portion of the doors in the form of a concentrated misty cloud. Because Master Rafik was fully aware of his journeyman Ekrem's clumsiness, he was constantly yelling and swearing, "Hey kid, you're screwing the whole thing up, look, do the lacquering right!" He was a such a pro, he could determine the lacquer concentration his journeyman sprayed on the doors from the force of the 'fiss' sound emitting from the spray gun. Journeyman Ekrem's dexterity was deteriorating fast with every expletive uttered by his master. Meanwhile, the red compressor pumping air for his lacquer gun came to his rescue. Once the air inside the compressor ran out, the propellor on top kicked in noisily. It was only the noise of the compressor that drowned out Master Rafik's blustery expletives. Of course, Journeyman Ekrem was swearing as well. However, he didn't blatantly shout obscenities at his master in order to get his weekly pay of 15 million TL. He swore inwardly to the high heavens.

- What the fuck's this Rafik shit? Rafik… Go screw yourself.

Journeyman Ekrem was quietly letting off steam by swearing at his master, whose name was written 'Rafik' on his identity card instead of 'Refik' due to a screw-up made at the census office. As for Munise and Leyla, they rolled out a carpet woven with curly embroideries onto the concrete floor, recoiling with the noise generated by Journeyman Ekrem and his abusive master, wriggling them out of their pensive thought. Giving their weepy eyes a brief recess, they began wondering about their new streets. What kind of world was behind their lime-stained windows? It wasn't only Master Rafik's pit saw or Journeyman Ekrem's lacquer spray gun that piqued their curiosity. Sounds of 'gijjjt gijjjt' began emitting from the garment workshop beneath the opposite apartment building. Neighborhood girls working in the garment industry in order to meet their dowry expenses ran pedalled knitting machines as they knitted sweaters and cardigans from giddy, nappy, fringed yarns. They'd knock on rolls of yarn as they pressed the play button on their double-cassette player while manually setting up the first left-and-right rounds on their machines. The voice of Hakkı Bulut booming from the cool looking tape deck with red and green lights fluctuating on every bass beat descended into the hidden corners of the street along with the morning sun.

From the sun, from the shade, from the blowing breezes

From every grain of soil you tread

From the string of white pearls around your neck

From the rosebuds you hold in your hand

From someone greeting you in passing

Whatever, I'm just jealous

Even I am jealous of myself

I've got a brother who's just three years old

Even I am jealous of him

The cassette in the player was a compilation. Every song featured voices and heavy words that released different feelings in the sweatshop girls. Hakkı Bulut's song of jealousy ended as Mahsun Kırmızıgül began to flatter himself beneath his moustache, as he sang, "If this is the World, I'm the King." By now, the girls were wide awake, chewing gum and reloading the gossip making the rounds in the neighborhood grapevine. As they accumulated their weekly wages, these girls had a few more skirts and blouses than girls who remained at home. They were in the sweatshop from 07:30 in the morning until 20:00 at night. That's why they were able to offer those dresses they wanted everyone to see while out gallivanting for each other's appraisal in that 20-m2 sweatshop. Like the machinery in front of them, they were on their feet until night. As the machine yanked the piece on top to the left and right, the sweater or cardigan overran from the lower part of the sweater loom as the machine incessantly made gıjjjt gıjjjt noises. The sweatshop's errand boy would collect the knitted pieces and stack the sleeves in one place and the read and front pieces in another place. The owner of the sweatshop, toothy Nergis began distributing sacks of these pieces to the women in the neighborhood. With every sack, she also gave beads with shiny sequins to be affixed to the sweater and cardigan pieces. She was paying 2000 lira per sweater and 2500 lira per cardigan embellished with beads and sequins. The neighborhood women earned their weekly market money from these beads and sequins.

While the door window glass trembled from toothy Nergis' side-splitting chuckles, who was gossiping with one of the working girls in front of the door, Leyla also got up to put brew a pot of tea. She filled the blue zinc teapot with water from the small sink at the toilet entrance, then placed it on top of the small gas tank. She lit the tank with a lighter she asked from Abdurrahman. She was going to prepare some things for breakfast. She removed cheese, olives and tomatoes from copper pots. The fridge was empty as the truck driver, Bahattin told them while moving everything inside, "Don't plug in the fridge for at least a day as it may break down." They were going to eat whatever they had. There was also some comb honey. Dirty Seref's wife, Halime gave it to them while they loaded their belongings onto the truck in Silvan. Munise and Leyla were quite surprised by this gift of Halime, the same Halime who didn't drop by if there wasn't any bairam or funeral ceremony. To their surprise, though she didn't come knocking much, Dirty Seref's wife Halime loved her neighbors to the extent of sharing the most valuable food in her kitchen. While she placed a piece of honey on her plate, she thought of Halime. If only Halime, who alway found an excuse not to stop by for a visit, had been with them and sat at their table together and dip bread in her honey together. They would have forgotten their unfamiliarities, even if it was for a little bit. Right when they were thinking of these points, her ear was distracted by a voice coming from the sweatshop.

"The magnolia is the most delicate flower

The magnolia is the most confidential of lovers

I'll love you an eyeful without your touch, too

Don't be sad, don't fade away, don't grieve, my magnolia"

Ali İbicek's fine voice plunged into the young girl's heart like a sharp knife.

His yearning for Leyla swelled mountainously in every magnolia of that melancholic tune, he was the vast sea that poured once more into her eyes...

- What are you doing here so early in the morning, Yılmaz?

- Uncle, I came here to see how my aunt was.

- Shut up boy, don't you think it's a bit early?

Uncle Halil was outraged seeing Yılmaz next to his cousins. He knew quite well that Yılmaz was one dodgy kid, to say the least. He regretted telling eager beaver Yılmaz that his cousins moved to İstanbul. God only knew what kind of shit he was involved in that made him drop by here. Munise and her children didn't even notice the tension between the uncle and nephew. They were busy hugging Hatice, fulfilling their yearning as if they had been apart for a millennium instead of a night.

Yılmaz realized he was going nowhere fast here as he grudgingly got to his feet, saying he work to do. In not waiting for breakfast despite all his aunt's objections, he took one final look at Leyla and exited the premises. He walked breathessly. He was totally incensed. In fact, he wanted to take the chipping hatchet propped up next to the sack of flour and smash it into his uncle's skull. Humiliated in front of Leyla ired him to no end. Frothing at the mouth like a rabid mutt, saying, "This pimp is going to get in the way of me getting married to Leyla as he poured on the obscenities.

While Leyla prepared the breakfast, Munise picked up her broom and dipper, then filled her bucket with water. It was her custom to wash down the front of her home every morning. Though she had a tough time accepting it, this shop was now her home and she needed to keep its doorway clean. She trudged over to the door of the shop that was a poor excuse for a home. She hadn't cast her eyes along the street as her stuff was being unloaded from the truck. Now she wondered what kind of place they had moved into. She opened the door slowly. The first scene she encountered was a woman smoking a cigarette and wearing a red- and black-striped bathrobe in front of the door as she laughed loudly with a frivilous girl. She was facing Toothy Nergis. Toothy Nergis lived in the floor over her sweatshop. She'd come into the sweatshop wearing her bathrobe. She enjoyed puffing on a smoke in front of the door after distributing her work amongst the neighborhood women. One couldn't call her a man in this state, and she didn't resemble a woman at all.

- Welcome neighbor

- Hey, I'm talking to you girl, welcome

- Don't you hear me, girl, are you deaf or what?

Munise was petrified. She was hearing Toothy Nergis. While she sort of understood what she said, she couldn't quite respond. What was she going to say now? She didn't speak Turkish … She finally uttered, "Peace be upon you." Taking a puff from her cigarette in the manner of a roughneck, the smoke drew into her lungs, coming out her nose as Toothy Nergis replied halfheartedly, "Peace be upon you, too." She then queried, "Hey neighbor, how did you end up in this God forsaken neighborhood?" Then it was back to square one. Munise was petrified as Toothy Nergis went bonkers… Munise looked and saw she was getting nowhere so she turned around. Her pulse rate accelerated but it was as if the blood in her veins wasn't flowing. She was indecisive, her emotions got caught up in on another. She was on the verge of both crying and chucking the bucket she held through the wide lime-covered window. She made eye contact with her Hatice. Mumbling a consoling religious phrase, she then took a deep breath. She didn't want to appear wretched in front of her youngest daughter. She said in Kurdish, "C'mon sweetheart, why don't you sweep the doorway?"… Hatice took the pail from her mother's hand. It was a bit heavy, but she enjoyed doing household chores. She went outside. The broom with its yellow handle held on with rusty wire and the pink dipper was at the edge of the door. First, she watered in front of their new home. She drew semi-circles with the water on the asphalt. She picked up the broom, bent over and began sweeping the street. Toothy Nergis was nowhere to be seen. From the sound of the chuckling coming from the top floor, she must have gone home. The carpentry journeyman Ekrem continued to lacquer his doors just a few meters beyond her, while the garment girls were chewing gum and gossiping over the clattering "gıjjt gıjjt" noise. While sweeping down the street, Hatice was curiously checking out the happenings around her. She wondered why nobody was sweeping in front of their doorways. When in fact, everyone in her old neighborhood would sweep their doorway clean early in the morning. The first conversation of the day was made while they held brooms in their hands. Just then, a noisy piece of wood passed in front of her that drowned out the sound of the lacquer spray gun. There was a blond kid on top with three steel ball bearings beneath it. Pushing the contraption from behind was a chubby kid his belly bulging from beneath his T-shirt, with wornout flip-flops on his feet. Because his hair color made people forget his name, the boy known on the street as 'blondie' constantly shouted "push faster, buddy, push faster," as the panting noise coming from chubby rivalled that coming from the ball bearings. The feet of the blond boy with the elfish face were on top of the slat attached in front of the board that made enough noise to bring the street down. He steered the board he sat atop by moving the slat left or right. Fashioned from throwaway pieces of wood the carpenter journeyman Ekrem gave the neighborhood kids, this ghetto skateboard was normally a two-seater on downhill streets. It turned into a pusher single-seat vehicle on flat streets. Chubby and the blond kid passed quickly in front of Hatice. The reason for their acceleration was not to reach the peak of excitement. Their problem was to save their asses from Infidel Makbule who lived at the top of the street. If she heard the commotion and came out onto her balcony, the entire street was going to hear just what bastards they were from Infidel Makbule's mouth.

Infidel Makbule had gotten so fed up, all the kids playing in the street suffered the verbal anguish of her expletives and physical abuse of her slippers aimed at their heads from the balcony. Infidel Makbule was a sour old witch who was never kind to children. She acquired the nickname 'Infidel Makbule' from swearing at children and adults alike, calling them 'infidel bastards". Anyways, chubby and blondie escaped the banshee wrath of Infidel Makbule without getting caught. They saved their asses, but Infidel Makbule, who couldn't make it to her balcony lickety-split as she was in the bathroom, found herself two victims the moment she emerged into the ether. The terrace of the opposite building was at an equal distance with Infidel Makbule's balcony. Two of the kids jumping from terrace to terrace while playing a morning session of hide-and-seek were crouched down in a corner. However, the reason for their perching on the terrace had nothing to do with hide-and-seek. The flappy-eared kid was toothy Nergis' boy, while the skinny one was the son of nightshift security guard Ekrem, who lived in the bungalow at the top of the street. The boys didn't go by their really names in the neighborhood, one was called 'Flappy,' and the other one was 'Bones.' They were ogling the porn magazine they'd swiped from the cabinet of the 'hood's fearless youngblood, barber Tayfun. They both felt ecstatic in capturing the source of the hot bed stories they heard from Barber Tayfun. Their eyes bugged out as they turned the pages, they dream worlds dashed from position to position. They had gotten so engrossed with the bullshit sex stories that flowed next to the unimaginable positions that made them say, "Hey, check this out!" they didn't even notice the ear-splitting din generated down below by chubby and blondie. Any other time and the two would've run on down to the street to commandeer a ride of their own. However, they had no intention whatsoever of interrupting this first experience they were tasting in the name of sexuality.

- You infidel bastards, go on, get the fuck outta there. You're perched there like crows, what the hell are you doing there?

The entire neighborhood could've caught fire for all they were concerned. They had their backs to the flames and were so caught up in the rapture just so they could turn one more page, when the boys leapt up as if they had pins and needles stuck up their butts. Their mag tumbled from their hands, vectoring in the air as it slowly landed next to their feet. Flappy quickly regained his wits as he deftly grabbed the magazine, and stuck it down his elastic underwear. He then pulled his T-shirt over it so nobody would notice, then they began their escape. They scrambled over the 50-centimeter high brick wall and made it over to the adjacent terrace. Then they opened the unlocked roof door and dived inside. They flew down the stairs, two by two and came out onto the street. Infidel Makbule was still on her balcony yelling "you infidel bastards." Flappy and Bones walked nonchalantly down the street as though they had nothing to do with Infidel Makbule's hollering that reverberated off the walls. They tried covering up the anxiety on their faces as they spotted Hatice, whom they were seeing on the street for the first time. They were lucky actually because Infidel Makbule had no idea what they were doing. She didn't need to understand anything to scold kids. Infidel Makbule was continuing to rant and rave from her balcony as Flappy and Bones crept into their bathrooms the instant they entered their homes.

Of those who were within hearing range along the entire street, Infidel Makbule's nerve-racking muttering only served to frighten Hatice. The silence of the street residents was because nobody wanted to get stabbed by the horns while dealing with the bull. Hatice didn't even bother to turn her eyes in the direction of Infidel Makbule's balcony. Out of fear, she put herself back on autopilot mode. She was going back and forther with the broom held in one of her hands. Her other hand was on her aching hips. The sun was glaring overhead… The sun darkened sometime later and a shadow descended over her. Hatice cringed. What would've happened if the ranting old lady breathed down her neck? She slowly straightened up like a timid kitten. As she stood up, she finely contemplated her body that the sun covered up. White sports shoes with untied laces wornout from playing ball, ice-blue jean pants with faded knees, a black T-shirt printed with a cartoon character… a pair of deep blue eyes… a pair of deep blue eyes, as intense as the sea she saw passing over the bridge… A face that was sunnier than the sun that blinded his body …

- I'm Sitki... Sidkullah... Forgive me Allah!

✳

03:27AM

-Shall we pour water on his face, dude??

- No way, dude, I don't think it'll make any difference if you poured a whole pail on him. A couple of whopping slaps on the face would do the trick though.

- Don't slap me, man, don't slap me…

I was like a trash bag piled up in front of a department store waiting for the municipality garbage truck to take me away. Though I couldn't get any part of my body to move, my memory was intact to the extent it was extracting the past from the depths of my inebriated brain. While I was imagining the sunny morning I met my Hatice and enjoying those days of yore, I was now driven down an entirely different abyss of my subconscious with a word which descended into my ear like a slap in the face. Every letter of the word 'slap' created the effect of a political rally loudspeaker embedded next to my eardrum. As the voice reverberating in my ear descended into my head like a well-aimed fist, my eyelids, which I couldn't budge until that moment, opened as wide as they could. I guess I transferred all my energy to my eyes, as I was barely able to say, "Don't slap me, dude." Standing over me now were two lowlifes, who had probably taken a stroll along İstiklal Avenue out of boredom, looking for girls to diss. While trying to figure out what these porcupine-heads looked like exactly, I wanted to say, "If you were cool, you'd have called 112 by now, bitch, what the hell are you talking about," but I didn't have enough strength to put together such a long sentence. These porcupine heads didn't give a shit about helping anyone anyway. It was clear they were looking for fun. Their idea of fun was no different than punks squirting a stray dog with water then driving it into some remote corner. While the poor dog was dealing with the water shock treatment, these two scumbags were physically five or ten years older than little monster brats who chortled as they hurtled kicks and jumped on the back of the scared shitless animal as if on horseback... They were also treating me like a soaked dog. Right up until a charming girl emitting a fine odor around her passed behind them. The minds of the two scumbags who could see a girl of that beauty only in the high-society pages of daily newspapers mixed with the fine scent and blown into the air. How could they not have been blown away? Once they saw her straight jet-black hair scattering in flight with the effect of her high heels, and flawless legs that undulated her pleated knee-high skirt with

every step she took, they were worse than dropping pills…
There wasn't anybody with the girl so It was impossible for
them to pass up this opportunity. These numbskulls could
only touch girls who had boyfriends next to them on this
avenue on New Year's Eve. So, they forgot about me and
promptly went after the babe instead… They sauntered off
in comfort provided by the crotch of their market stall-grade
denim pants that came down to their kneecaps. It was as
if the two of them were aware they wouldn't be able to get
much closer than chatting distance with such a girl any time
in their lives. And the two were just thinking about chatting
her up at the very least, and if possible, fondle her up in a
secluded corner.

I was still jittery. Yet, around the time I mumbled "Don't
slap me, dude," the two porcupine heads had long caught up
to the pearl white neck of the pleasant smelling girl whose
noses were darkened with black blemishes. I think they
found the courage to pinch the nice smelling girl's thighs
or boobs when they reached a street corner off the avenue
that opened into pitch darkness. I understood even from
the vibrating lamp posts illuminating the avenue that the
nice scented girl had shrieked, "Help Police!" The audacious
courage of the porcupine headed scumbags turned to
unfettered fear that frightened them to death as they booked
it out of there. They had left but I was still scared of getting
slapped. My brain had a tough time issuing a command
to my hands to shut my face. Dammit, even while I was
unconscious, I was afraid of being slapped. When in fact

I knew from my childhood before getting into a rumble, the tough boys in the neighborhood would take pills if they could find them, if not, grass, and if they couldn't find that, then they'd down a case of beer. If that wasn't available, they'd fill their lungs with paint thinner fumes swiped from the car paintshop in the upper neighborhood, then head out. Their greatest weapon would be their high-as-a-kite heads. One of the bullies once said that those throwing a punch at someone stoned would only hurt themselves. Why am I any different dammit it?! Even while I'm stoned, the possibility of being slapped drives me crazy. I might be able to bear it if they break my legs or slash my arms, but never could I endure a slap in the face… This is such a fear that if they were to Wheel me into the operating ward and put me under general anesthesia, nothing extra was needed for me to regain consciousness. I swear, I'd leap to my feet with just one slap. But even while I'm high, I remember the reason for my fear of being slapped. This was the souvenir of the bearded son of a bitch. The SON of a BITCH.

It was impossible for me to forget that day. It was a Sunday in the spring of 1995, the last day in April… We played just played a match with the Backstreet Boyz and were on the way home. I had Flappy on my right, Bones on my left, Blondie next to him, with Chubby taking up the rear… Flushed with the pride of handing the Backstreet Boyz a loss after such a long time, we were shoving the ball forward as we advanced towards our street. It was really miraculous, but Chubby did a fantastic job as a goalkeeper, in that he only gave away four goals. One was between the legs, but anyways… This time, the foul-mouthed kids on the back street didn't talk the freebie goal malarky like they did in the other games. While we agreed half-time would be at "five goals and the game would be over at 10," they had no idea they'd be giving up 10 goals so quickly during the first 20 minutes. Because they started a row, blaming each other for the defeat, the freebie Chubby gave up sort of slipped by the wayside. Even though Flappy got on Chubby's case, saying, "We won, so why'd you have to go and give up the freebie?", it was still a glorious day for the Chubster. He chested several potential goals and with some unexpected agility from his fat ass, even caught a few balls that were headed into the corner. He was sniping at us from behind as if to avenge the agony of being called 'Barrelhead' in previous matches. We were all laughing as we entered our street, posing like Arnold Schwarzenegger stepping out in front of balls of fire after blowing up some warehouse filled with bad guys. We passed in front of the cobbler at the corner, feeling as mighty as Conan and indestructible as The Terminator.

The resounding 'tock, tock' noise made by Cobbler Recep as he hammered the wooden sole of a shoe jammed between his legs became the sweet rhythm for our swaggering steps we took in moments we got really carried away in the 'yo, whatssupwidat' role. Rivulets of sweat seeping from our school-style crewcuts along with the blowing breeze rolled from our necks to our backs, cooling us down. The Feel Good Gang felt on top of the world. I was the one who named the gang. We formed the gang with such good feelings that we didn't dare tell anyone we were a gang for fear of getting the other neighborhood gangs to turn on us. In short, we didn't relish fights…

- Come on over here, you rugrats!

- Get over here, you bunch of little scoundrels!

The sweet rhythm in our steps was knocked askew like a broken record while passing in front of Master Rafik's property filled with timber boards. An association had opened about four or five months ago in the building adjacent to the property where kids played marbles in the dirt and dust in the spaces not occupied by the timber. The voice was coming from there. Chubby was the first to cringe from Mule Nevzat's raspy voice. He shook off the armor of a victorious commander protecting his goal post and reverted back to his old self in a navy blue sweat suit with two torn knees and Velcro-fastened white sneakers bulging at the sides. He took two quick steps forward and quietly whispered in my ear from behind: "Siti, what the fuck does this Mule faggot want?" Chubby was the only one who called me 'Siti' without me getting angry. He was obliged to whisper his question regarding Mule Nevzat. Especially if it was a question that stressed Mule's queerness… Chubby and I and the entire neighborhood knew Mule Nevzat quite well. He'd opened his shirt buttons practically down to his belt, and wear pointy-toed shoes, and go to and fro to the neighborhood police station every other day because he was constantly getting in fights. At times he didn't get in brawls, he'd confront kids on their way to school, extort 'pretzel and soda' money from them and give most of them a slap on the face for good measure. There wasn't a kid in the neighborhood who could get through junior-high school without getting slapped by Mule Nevzat. With the exception of tough bros who were strong enough to give Mule a taste of his own medicine..

There was no way the kids could rid themselves of Mule even if school had been out. This time, he'd hang out at the corner shop where the kids worked the counter. He wouldn't pay for the ice-cream he took, and wouldn't leave the shop without filling his pockets with a handful of munchies. Of course, this was when he was being nice. There were other times when he scooped 2000-lira worth of ice-cream, snapping at the kid who asked for money, "I gave you 10,000 lira, give me my change. He'd swear, rant and rave and wouldn't leave the shop without pocketing 8000 TL. He'd buy some phone tokens with this money and sprint to the telephone booth. As if chatting up and fondling women on the street wasn't enough, he'd harrass them on the phone as well. He'd dial numbers until he ran out of tokens he'd steal from the post office, hanging up on some of them with an 'offff' and others with a "fuck off bitch."

Some time later, it was as if the world began spinning backwards as something happened to Mule Nevzat. 1995 passed like an April Fool's joke… He added a hairy red beard to his freckled face. He stopped wandering around with an open chest area and switched to crew neck shirts buttoned up to the final button and always seemed to be wearing baggy trousers. He began going back and forth to the association with a brown agenda stuck under his armpit. He got used to walking with a contorted neck. Mule Nevzat was the epitome of the 'I've seen the light' message which gradually transformed him into Nevzat Hodja in front of the entire neighborhood. By now, he had attained the position where he could say, "Well, if you're not like us, then you're all infidels." It didn't take him a long time to reach this level. The categorization of 'those who don't vote for us are from the potato religion' which lowered the language of trashy politics onto the street, made Mule's work so much easier. Moreover, Mule had selected the easiest target again. Once again, there was no peace of mind for the kids in the neighborhood. With this new Nevzat Hodja image, none of them had the chance to even say "Looks like that faggot Mule is outta our hair." He would smack the seal of approval ('Moslem son') or disapproval ('infidel twerp') on their foreheads so fast, it would make their heads spin. And with such great pleasure not to be had even on days when he'd bash them to Kingdom Come.

- Hey asshole, why aren't you coming to the association?

- Why should I come?

- What, are you a fuckin' infidel or what? You better Show up, you fuck.

- I'm not an infidel, Thank Allah I'm a Moslem.

- If you're a Moslem, why don't you come, motherfucker? This is the association for those who live the Moslem way.

- Why, you think the only Moslem are those who go to the association?

- Hey bitch, don't be ridiculous. Choose your place. Look at all the infidels dying. They'll all end like those in Oklomo.

Mule couldn't say 'Oklahoma.' One couldn't expect perfect pronunciation from someone who had a tough time saying a maximum 35 words per day, not including expletives of course. Anyways, nobody made a big deal about this pronunciation slip up. As a matter of fact, none of the kids had a clue as to what 'Oklomo' meant. But I knew quite well what he was trying to say. I had watched it on the news a week ago. A bomb blew up in front of a building in Oklahoma and more than 150 people died. I was really downhearted about that. I mean, I couldn't accept death other than those that occur on natural expiry dates. Such death is an end that nobody deserves. There was no way I could expect this sensibility from Mule, who was so devoid of life, he rather rummages through the pockets of an elderly for money than shed tears for a dying father, Besides, I wasn't as naive as he thought. But I wanted to make Mule feel like he was a rotten apple.

- Why do you call everyone infidels? Who knows, maybe there are some believer amongst them. Besides, even if they weren't Moslem, why should they have to die?

- Dude, they're infidels. They're all bastards. They should all die.

- How do you know they're bastards? Alright, fine, let's say they're all a bunch of bastards, wouldn't their mothers cry for their poor souls?

Mule lost all sense of self-control. He had a hard time dealing with humanity for as long as I've known him. Once he realized he couldn't pronounce 'Oklahoma' right, he began foaming at the mouth. Had he been his previous version, he would've cussed me out as he slapped me around to Hell and back. He now sported a beard over his baggy trousers and he had reached the rank of lining everyone up at the central mosque, where he used to go only to use the toilet to discharge the beer from his bladder. Barking out the command, 'Keep the lines tight,' sometimes he'd have the empty spaces in the front rows filled by harsh hand motions, while other times with verbal orders, then he'd commence the prayer ritual. He was the star performer of the congregation. Consequently, he wouldn't have undermined his new image by swearing in front of everyone. But I was obliged to pay the price for catching him so off guard in front of everyone. Without further ago, he drew his weapon in order not to be further humiliated. He filled the clip with 'I'm Moslem, everyone else is an infidel" jargon. This parlance sold like hotcakes back then. Then he started firing…

- Whadya think you're saying, punk! Why don't you come by and learn a few words from the Quran? What are you, a follower of the potatoes religion?

- First of all, I memorized the Quran way back when I was in first grade. My father taught me. So why don't you learn it first.

- You don't know shit. You're lying out your crack. Recite the 'elham.'

- You recite it first.

- I'm gonna kill you dude, you think you can outdo me?

- Tell you what, you recite the rules of recitation, I'll follow with the entire Ya-sin surah. Okay, are you ready?

I was seriously going to recite the Yasin surah, but I didn't even have the chance to say "Ya." Not knowing even what the rules of recitation meant, a thoroughly incensed Mule landed an awkward blow on my left cheek. In addition to the unbearable pain trickling from my cheek down to my chest, the valves of my nose which bleed at the slightest touch, opened full blast. Blood gushing from my nostrils ran down from my lips to my neck and then flowed onto my sweaty T-shirt. I guess this is what it means to be left in blood and sweat… Then again, I didn't remain idle… The moment I took the blow to my face, I shouted in pain, "Allah" as I swung a kick. Unfortunately, my kick caught up in Mule's baggy trousers and didn't reach the target. Throwing his big butt backwards to get away from the kick's impact, Mule launched another slap in my direction. He couldn't connect. Despite my painful nose, I turned quickly to the side, as Mule's awkward hand grazed my back. During that drifting motion, blood flowing from my nose drew a crimson semi-circle in the asphalt with a curved skidding movement. Not able to tolerate the thrashing I received, Chubby wanted to get in a shot at Mule. Of course nobody could do this to the leader of Feel Good Gang. Fine, nobody was going to get in a fight, but nobody was also going to take a hit. Seeing the hatred on Bones and Flappy's faces, who were looking for a chance to jump on Mule's back, I ignored the pain in my nose and stopped Chubby from lunging. Otherwise, Mule would have left me alone and jumped the three of them at once. Perhaps Cobbler Recep would come running to help break up the fracas. That said, this Mule was no different than an antagonized rabid bitch, so the coldhearted bum would've most likely beaten up Grandpa Recep as well.

I grabbed Chubby by the arm and saying "C'mon, let's go!" began dragging him homeward. I also motioned with my head for Bones and Flappy to fall in behind. While walking, I swore a blue streak at Mule. The more the blood wouldn't stop running from my nose, the more I got more pissed off. I said, "I shit on your beard," and instantly regretted it. I got a guilty conscience cursing his foot-long beard he grew to appear religious, hitting me hard, like an elephant. So much so, the beard was the sunnah of our Master Prophet. I had just sworn at circumcision. I hurt so badly in my heart. While cleaning my nose with the bottom part of my T-shirt, I gave myself the opportunity to do a little reckoning. I pondered… Sauntering pensively at my side with the dream of beating up Mule, I uttered, "I shit on your beard" in a tone that brought Chubby out of his daydream. Why should I have a guilty conscience? I wasn't swearing at circumcision… I was only swearing at some dickhead punk who understands it's a prick with its end snipped off when he hears the word 'circumcision.' If that punk knew about the Prophet and his sunnah, would he feel so thrilled about killing people? Man, my father told me that the Prophet Muhammed didn't want to wake up a cat sleeping on his frock, so he cut the edge of the frock from where he sat, then got up. What would the faggot Mule understand about the sunnah of the Prophet, who didn't even deny animals the compassion that people don't show each other! Of course, he'd understand absolutely diddly-squat. I'm at peace, and the guilty feeling that gnawed at my conscience had flown off like a bird. I shit on your beard, Mule. Right in the very middle of it…

- Who the hell opened this association here? What made them come to this street, Sıtı?

- Fuck it!

My intention was to for-fucking-get about it, but that was not to happen when Chubby took a few steps and answered his own question, muttering, "They're going to make us Moslems." This wasn't his own determination. I also heard this sentence at the association, which had become the new bane of our lives. I recall they held a knowledge contest there when it first opened. They had a neighborhood resident line up some plastic chairs and they had a few kids sit at some tables. While the downstairs filled with women, those upstairs were following the proceedings via a camera linked into the television. I was also amongst the viewers upstairs. They called it a knowledge quiz, but the questions were weird. I mean, I was either very ignorant or else these guys' concept of knowledge was very different. I was expecting them to consider the age group of the kids competing in the contest and ask questions from their history, geography lessons taught at junior-high school, or from story books. I was bewildered. If I huffed and puffed out of exasperation, the crowd kept me from even getting up from where I sat, let alone going outside… I was really acerbated by the final boring chatter of the young man holding a microphone as he asked questions and tried to be humorous at the same time. He was asking the name of a writer. It was clear the person he asked was one of the writers Moslems cared about wanting to make Moslem once again. While counting off one by one what this writer had written, to whom he gave lessons, and all tough times he went through in life, the young presenter ended his question regarding the writer by smirkingly saying, "Now he lives in Europe." I looked at the adolescent contestants and they all drew a blank. They were furtively eyeing each other. Seeing the kids squirming about uncomfortably, the presenter got really fired up with his gagging punchline. "How could you not know him, kids, he lives in Europe, on the European side of Istanbul…"

- Screw your sense of humor!

"Sense of humor" was one of the few expressions in English I knew. I learned it from my rosy-lipped teacher named Nevin at an English-language course I was enrolled in. Because I purchased a set of English-language books, I had the privilege to participate in a month of free weekend lessons. I had made a couple of jokes that were on par with those of the presenter at the association, which led the rosy-lipped teacher to remark, "You have a good sense of humor." I can still feel the warm breeze on her face when she said the Turkish meaning. Repeating the words that emerged between her crimson lips, I jotted them down letter by letter in my notebook. "You have a good sense of humor!" I learned the meaning of each word. I could've learned a lot more from the rosy-lipped teacher. Although teacher Nevin never wore lipstick, if only I had focused on what she wrote on the blackboard rather than her ruddy lips… I preferred her red lips. This sentence is the only thing remaining from that month of lessons. I was now putting the product of that sweet memory to use in cussing out the bullshitting MC. Screw your sense of humor!

One of the association's assistants was sitting beside me. Anyways, he didn't understand what I said. As I huffed and puffed in frustration since the start of the contest, the guy next to me turned and said in a tone everyone could hear, "Look son, the guy's trying to make sure this district is Moslem, so what are you doing? So why don't you just straighten your act up, listen and try to learn something, jackass." I didn't care how everyone was leering at me. S everyone froze sheep-like where they were to see where that voice came from, I grabbed the opportunity to step over a few folks as I showed myself out. I encountered Master Rafık's journeyman Ekrem in front of the door, and grinned, "Our neighborhood is full of infidels, dude." While Ekrem tried to comprehend what he'd just heard, I added my infamous phrase, "Screw your sense of humor." Ekrem responded to the part he understood, "Go screw yourself!"

I cheered up while thinking back just how surprised Journeyman Ekrem was that day. However, I got peeved whenever I saw Tilelayer Muhsin strolling towards the association picking his nose as usual. I was really bent out of shape with this guy. Tilelayer Muhsin kept pace with the evolution Mule Nevzat went through. He used to constantly hang out in the coffee house on the back street, spending his entire life at the rummy-cube table. He had no worries such as finding work as he retired from his janitorial job before he turned 40. Because he hobnobbed with the rummy tiles all day long, he was known throughout the neighborhood as 'Tile Master.' There were occasions when he left the coffee house before nightfall and if he entered the street, he'd definitely find someone to bicker with. Tilelayer Muhsin and his wife Dark Nuriye were inevitably on one side of the argument that occurred on the street. Everyone knew this and made a concerted effort to avoid their paths. Like all wiggly characters in the neighborhood, Tilelayer Muhsin kept up with the social changes. His clothing and his manner of speech changed as he came and went from the association. He switched from wearing Cuban-heeled shoes to bathroom slippers all the time, saying it was more comfortable while performing ablutions, a point he'd bring up in all his conversations, whether it was relevant or not. He traded in his irregular moustache for a twisty beard, crew neck shirt and baggy trousers, all of which became an indispensable part of Tilelayer Muhsin's lifestyle. Nonetheless, this change reflecting in his outfits didn't rub off on his temperament. The only thing that changed about his grumpy, slimeball character was the way he instigated arguments. Nowadays, he didn't finish a single sentence without an innuendo about the piety of those living along our street to the tune of 'Brother, we're Moslems, thank Allah."

Tilelayer Muhsin was so religious, even the brand-new Renault 21 Manager everyone wondered how he was able to afford on his retirement pension was green. The money his wife Dark Nuriye made sewing party banners also wasn't enough for them to afford that car. Rumors about him had been running rampant since the day he took over the association's financial affairs. Tilelayer Muhsin would go on a rampage whenever the whereabouts of the donation funds was brought up. He'd gag people with his cliché, "What, does it bother you to know we're enrolling students so they can learn the Quran." It was precisely for this reason that he came to blows with Master Rafik. Master Rafik took a blow to the chest when he asked, "Lemme tell you something, I've been working like a dog for the past 25 years and I was barely able to afford an Anadol pickup truck, so tell me how you're able to afford that brand-new car of yours, Muhsin." There was another group in the neighborhood that believed Tilelayer Muhsin was involved in some dodgy business. But unlike Master Rafik, nobody ever broke their silence on the matter. They didn't want to sour the association's business, With the concern that "it would hinder benevolence," they went out of their way not to talk about Tilelayer Muhsin's great blunder. They believed that ratting on the evildoer would get in the way of goodness. It didn't occur to them that the best thing they could to be rid of evil would be to carry out goodness.

The hatred I harbored for Tilelayer Muhsin had nothing to do with his shady get-rich schemes. I didn't care whether he drove a brand-new car or even a Jetson's spaceship for that matter... I was bored at home on a weekend day and went out to get the gang together for a football match. They'd gone over to the association to watch a film and I unwillingly went there to round them up. Our gang was sitting on plastic chairs lined up in front of the television, their heads looking up at the wall-mounted television, watching an elderly person telling about whatever came to mind as he wandered through some mountainous countryside. There were a couple of kids from the back street amongst them as well. It was evident they were all bored but they had to be patient in order to watch a Kung-Fu film that was going to be inserted after this film. The precondition for watching the Kung Fu film was that they had to follow this ridiculous footage. I was right behind them. At first, none of them noticed me. I was distracted by slippers and a pair of small sports shoes at the door of the carpeted chat room. I didn't think much of it as I turned around to our gang and shouted in their midst, "Get up guys, let's go play a game." Chubby, Flappy, Bones and Blondie got to their feet simultaneously. After experiencing a bit of uncertainty between the Kung Fu film and the game, they said, "C'mon dude" as they shoved each other off the plastic chairs and got up. Just then, a kid jumped from the carpeted partition that was utilized as the association's chat room. It was Ramazan who lived on the street behind us. Ramazan was a small fry, in the third- or fourth-grade in elementary school. His mother remarried after his father died, and left the poor kid with his paternal grandmother. Ramazan was a shy kid who wouldn't cry if you beat him. His face and neck were beet red as he emerged from the room. While he hurriedly tried to put his shoes on, Tilelayer Muhsin appeared from behind him. He smacked the kid on his neck, saying, "You're a good wrestler kid, well done." That's when I realized something fishy had been going on inside. Tilelayer Muhsin had a filthy smirk on his face that didn't want to give away the filthiness he did on his face. Meanwhile, I looked at the kid's face. He looked horrifically at Tilelayer Muhsin as if to say, "What the hell did you do to me."

So, it meant the story spoken amongst our gang was true after all. I wanted to do in Tilelayer Muhsin that instant. Unfortunately, I wasn't in any condition to do anything at all. Had I gone out into the street and shouted, they wouldn't have believed me nor Ramazan. He had those famous slippers on his feet and persuasive words on his tongue. It wouldn't have even taken five minutes for Tilelayer Muhsin's friends and relatives to declare me an enemy of religion. Even had I taken out the cap I never neglected to put on while conducting obligatory prayers which I kept folded in my pocket and waved it around, they'd point out my American crew cut, say I was infidel seed and come on top again. The conditions were evident and it was impossible to fight them. The best thing was to refer Tilelayer Muhsin to Allah and stay clear of the association. That's what I did. I had the wretched Ramazan come in front of us as I removed our gang from the association. That was the last time I stepped inside that place. As he sprinted homewards, I never saw Ramazan again on our street.

While Tilelayer Muhsin sauntered past us with his finger up his nose and his mind on some innocent little kid, we encountered Toothy Nergis. She emerged in front of the door to gossip with one of the girls. Seeing me in my bloodied state, she took the cigarette in her mouth into her right hand, asking, "What happened, son?" as she reached her left hand to my cheek. "It's nothing, Aunt Nergis, I got smacked playing football." The ball in Flappy's hand was enough to convince Toothy Nergis. He wriggled our way out of Toothy Nergis' interrogation and entered the building that had no outer door. Chubby's home was on the floor right above the sweatshop. The owner of the building, Enver from Samsun lived above him. We quickly climbed the stairs and went onto the terrace without being seen by Chubby's mother. I went immediately over to the faucet on the terrace and removed my T-shirt. As was the case in many other buildings, Enver from Samsun had a non-metered water line hooked up onto the terrace. The plumber laid it out in such a way that not even the meter readers noticed the illegal pipe that reached the terrace from between the beams. Enver from Samsun forced his wife Sevgi to conduct all the household chores with the illegal water. The poor girl couldn't convince her husband that using this running water was wrong. Enver from Samsun considered it his right to use non-metered water. Everyone was using it, was he the only fool in the neighborhood? Of course he was going to use it…Getting all hung up on the illicit water to the point of constantly escaping the danger of drowning in her dreams, Aunt Sevgi was really ill at ease. Despite getting an earful of expletives from Enver of Samsun on the day the bill arrived, at least she was careful not to cook any food with the illicit water. I know this because she'd come over to our place and pour out all her troubles onto my mother.

I opened the faucet at the end of the illegal line and began to wash my navy blue T-shirt. I picked up the soap which was muddied on top next to the faucet. I rubbed the soap thoroughly into the T-shirt. The stains on both the soap and the T-shirt began to disappear. After rinsing and wringing it out completely, I spread the T-shirt to dry on top of the stove pipe. Flappy, Bones, Blondie and Chubby had already stretched out on the blanket on which Aunt Sevgi ha whipped fleece that morning. They opened up a space for me as well. The remaining pieces of wool that stuck to the blanket got mixed in their hair and got in their mouths. We got really drowsy as we gazed at our circling dreams in our eyelids that rotated a red curtain beneath the sunlight. Chubby was riding through the streets on a BMX bike with yellow tires, Flappy was having a blast in the bumper car ride at the nearby amusement park, Blondie was playing football on the street in full Number 9 Galatasaray regalia replete with leggings and shorts. Bones' curtain was a huge mess, as usual... There was a blood everywhere. He had a switchblade in his hand… He made a fist and stuck it between his thumb and pointer finger, supported it with his other fingers and wrist, with the sharp end protruding outwards... He had learned to hold it in a way that would only wound when he stabbed someone with it. It didn't strike deadly blows. He plunged the shiny, sharp tip into his father's flesh, so he'd learn a lesson not to beat his mother ever again. One to his thigh, one to his belly… One to his back, one to his head… Again and again… He wanted blood to spurt from everywhere just like his mother, distraught from all the physical abuse she took. Don't let him die, but don't let him beat my mother up anymore …

As usual, I dwelled on my black-eyed Hatice. I last spoke with my Hatice on this terrace. We had sat behind the terrace door clasping hands. I opened my eyes and looked at the spot where I sat with Hatice. Then I shut my eyes again. My Hatice had recently moved onto our street and I saw her pitch-dark eyes one morning while she was sweeping in front of her building. From that day onward, I'd run into the street at the same time of day in order to see those dark eyes of hers. After some time, Hatice got accustomed to both me and the street. It wasn't long before we not only started meeting early in the morning, but in the evening hours as well. Our evening meetups were very special. Once the summer coolness descended upon the street and it got a little dark outside we'd go up on the terrace without anyone seeing us. We always preferred this spot for our rendezvous as the apartment didn't have an outside door, making it easier for us. There was no need for anyone to open the door in order to go up to the terrace. We weren't afraid of being caught. We were trembling with the excitement of approaching at the distance of a warm breath. I was in my right mind, the blood my heart pumped was racing with the pressure of water released by the floodgates of a dam. Though we were shy during the early days, it wasn't long before we began holding hands every time we met. In fact, I even once planted a sweet kiss on Hatice's cheek. We wer both embarrassed. I get embarrassed every time I remember that moment. A pang of regret overcame me, "If only I had kissed her every time we met." Especially that final night... If only we had spoken longer, if only I had held her elegant hands longer, and kissed her to my heart's content... It hadn't even been two months since she moved to our street, how was I supposed to know that night was to be the last time I met with my dark-eyed one. Who could've guessed I was going to witness an unforgettable nightmare when men darker than the darkness that descended on the street were to take Hatice away that night? I squinted my eyes in the dazzling sun and returned to my dreams filled with Hatice on the wool blanket.

Hatice's departure...

Hatice and Sıdkullah came down from the terrace five minutes apart and went to their homes. After eating dinner and watching some TV, Sıdkullah had stretched out on his bed and was trying to sleep in the stifling heat of the night. First he heard the sound of a car, then noisy clamor. It was as if all hell had broken loose. He ran immediately to the balcony. His parent had even reached the balcony before him. Not just them, but the entire street was at their balconies or windows. The commotion was coming from Hatice's home. There was a car, a white Tempra, with its engine running at the front of their door. It was a new SLX model, with its tail in the air. There was someone in a black outfit waiting right next to the white car... Like the car he was waiting beside, his tail was also in the air. The hollering was getting louder and louder. Someone was crying. We heard a voice from one of the balconies, ""Hey you, What's going on there at this hour, what are you doing over there?" The voice was so wussy, nobody understood who was doing the talking other than the owner of the voice. The guy in the black suit waiting in front of the car took out a gun from his waist. After lifting his head aimlessly, and turned it this way and that, he shouted, "Stay out of it, get back in your homes, assholes, move it!" Just then, someone was making a racket in Hatice's home. Uninterrupted shrieks were heard. Hatice was in the arms of three dark men. She was screaming at the top of her lungs "Mother," while trying to free herself from their powerful arms. She coudn't even squirm in the burly men's arms. They tossed her tiny body into the back seat of the car like a can of peas in a shopping cart then they got in the car in no time flat. Munise and Leyla came flying out right behind them in their bare feet. Shouting and wailing, they stuck to the door handles. But as soon as the armed getaway man got behind the wheel and stepped on the gas, they both were dragged a few meters and left alone all black and blue in the middle of the street. Mother and daughter collapsed on the pavement, lamenting their loss. Munise wailed in Kurdish, "Leave my Hatice alone." "Help, they kidnapped my Hatice…" but nobody understood. As it was, most of those looking on from their balconies and windows had gone back inside out of fear. The troubles that made Munise flee her homeland were back with a vengeance in İstanbul. While she feared they were going to abduct her only son Abdurrahman with the white Renault Toros, they took away her black-eyed little one in a white Tempra. Once again, they fashioned a handkerchief from their white muslin headcovers.

The moment the white Tempra was lost from sight, the neighbors hiding in their homes began to come down to the street one by one. Sıdkullah had already gone by Munise and Leyla's side. In fact, he was the third person along with the mother and daughter who went chasing after the Tempra. He didn't even hear his father shouting from the balcony, "Get your butt back home." Like cruel monsters, the folks on the street had descended over the mother and daughter, crying their eyeballs out as they sat on the pavement. Mouths that were too scared to utter a single word a few minutes ago were asking questions like, "Who were they, were those guys your relatives, why did they kidnap the girl …", puncturing Munise's heart like a spinning drill bit. Her limbs were frozen beneath a lifeless street lamp glued to the electric post, as the blood pumped from her heart refused to circulate through her weary body. She was in such pain that she didn't even notice Leyla, who was sitting beside her, had just fainted and was lying prone on the asphalt. Sıdkullah's mother Emine together with Enver of Samsun's wife, Sevgi were trying to resuscitate the young girl in the midst of the buzzing crowd. They tried slapping her face, which was injured as she fell to the ground, but to no avail. Sidkullah had gone home without anyone noticing and lunged breathlessly back into the street holding a pitcher of water. He had taken his second step when he smacked into someone with long hair wearing a suit. Half of the water in the pitcher had spilled onto that guy. He was worried he might've been one of Hatice's abductors. The guy in the suit he smacked into was none other than Yılmaz. Abdurrahman was also next to him.

After having a fish sandwich in Eminönü and strolling around the sites in the area, they had come to the bottom of the street in a joyful mood. Once they saw the crowd in front of the home, they began to walk anxiously. Yılmaz's haste was interrupted by Sıdkullah and the water in his pitcher. Abdurrahman breathlessly ran over next to his mother. He started crying when he saw his sister lying on the ground. Meanwhile, he was asking his mother what had happened, partly in Turkish and partly in Kurdish…

Shaking off his nervousness, Sıdkullah plunged into the middle of the crowd and handed the half-filled water pitcher to his mother. Seeing Leyla's unconscious body in the hands of the neighborhood, Yılmaz stepped loudly into the crowd. Leyla's head was on Yılmaz's knees. Just then, Sıdkullah's mother tipped the half-pitcher on Leyla's face. The young girl's lilac-colored, handmade head covering got mixed in the water, slipped from her black hair and fell to the ground. Yılmaz's gray jacket which had just gotten wet, became thoroughly drenched. Of course, Yılmaz wasn't concerned … He asked his aunt what had happened without taking his eyes off Leyla. While Munise pressed her son Abdurrahman against her bosom and wept, she told in vivid detail how

Hatice was abducted by three armed men as though it was happening all over again. In raiding their mutated shop of a home while she was drinking tea with her daughters, they entered by kicking in the door, which they left opened slightly in order for air to enter their mildew-smelling home. They were two people, one was an old man with a single tooth remaining and the other was of Yılmaz's build with a crooked nose... They removed weapons from their waists and aimed them at Munise and her daughters, who froze in fear. They swore as they kicked some household items. Once they couldn't find much else to kick, they began digging the pointed toes of their high-heeled shoes into Munise and Leyla. Writhing in pain, Leyla was able to ask, "What do you want?" The old man with the single remaining tooth answered with a kick instead of his mouth. Then he grabbed Hatice by the wrist and pulled her towards himself, as he got her to stand up. He started dragging her towards the door. Leyla disregarded the pain from the kicks jabbing her head and latched onto her sister's ankle. Hatice's wrist was in hand of the old man with the single remaining tooth while her ankle was in her sister's hand... She was squirming to save her life... Munise also motioned to grab Hatice but the lout with the crooked nose kicked her so hard she couldn't budge from her place. She had the wind knocked out of her. In trying to rid himself of Leyla, the old man with the single remaining tooth swung consecutive kicks at her in order to get Hatice outside. In putting up a struggle up to the foot of the door, Leyla was forced to loosen her grip on Hatice's ankle due to the debilitating kick blows. Meanwhile, Munise had regained her composure and had gotten up to rescue her Hatice from the hands of the old man. Shrieking at the top of her lungs, she charged towards the door. The lout with the crooked nose gave her one more swift kick while bundling the girl into the back of the car. In a final desperate attempt, Leyla reached her arm inside the car's open window. The old man gnawed Leyla's hand with his single tooth. Feeling a pain not unlike a pinprick, Leyla didn't give up as she gripped the window with her other hand. Munise also clung to the half-open window. As they clung tightly, they thought they were going to be able to stop the car. The boy across the street was struggling to open the car's rear door and was slamming his fists onto the glass, which was completely closed. May Allah bless him, he was the neighbor's son. Once the car went into motion, the three of them were thrown to the asphalt a few meters further down.

Munise's anguished narrative of events also answered the questions of the neighbors who towered over them. But Munise explained everything in a language that was quite foreign from the one everyone heard here every day. The curiosity of the neighbors had piqued considerably, but hearing the old man with the single tooth, Yılmaz understood what had happened. For sure, it was the old bastard at the tavern who raided the home. "Fine, but how did he find this place? The son of a bitch must have been following me."

Once Leyla began to regain her wits, they carried mother and daughter into their home. The teapot was overturned, glasses were broken and everything was in disarray. Abdurrahman hurriedly straightened up the mattresses. They had the mother and daughter sit on the mattresses. Sıdkullah's mother Emine also set the teapot up in a corner. Neighbor Emine folded the carpet with broken glass all over it, dragged it into a corner. While the other women were dealing with the mother and daughter, they were also examining the nooks and crannies of the home they'd entered. Because none of them had even called on the family that came from Silvan to take refuge in this shop in an effort to welcome them to the neighborhood. With the exception of Emine and Sevgi... As it was, of the neighbors who ventured inside, only these two were tending to the mother and daughter. The others were only concerned about ridding their curiosity about this mysterious family.

Yılmaz grasped the hand of her weeping aunt, saying, "I'm going to bring Hatice back, I swear." He looked at Leyla and uttered once more, "I promise as Allah is my witness." As he got to his feet angrily, his hand went down to his hip to feel for his gun. Abdurrahman then stood up as well.

- Bro, who are these guys, where did they take my sister, for God's sake?

- I'm going to get Hatice, don't you worry, I'm going to get those bastards, dead or alive ...

- C'mon, bro, let's go wherever we're going before something happens to my sister.

- You're not coming, stay here.

- What are you saying, bro, you can arrange a piece for me, too.

- Dude, don't leave your mother and sister alone, I said I was going to take care of it.

- No way, bro, that's my sister we're talking about, how could I stay here?

- Then get moving, we're going to stop by my place first.

- Bro, what does your place have to do with this, c'mon, let's go wherever we have to go.

- Don't talk so much, Abdurrahman, get moving…

They got up and left. Sıdkullah was also eager to go together with them. He was leery of his mother. What was he going to say, how was he going to account for his behavior? How was he going to say he loved Hatice? Everyone was already astonished he was dragged chasing the car. Because all attention was on Munise and Leyla for the time being, he had yet to deal with their inquisitive questions. Still, he didn't remain inside and went out in front of the door. One by one, the curious neighbors followed suit. His mother and Enver of Samsun's wife, Sevgi were the only ones remaining inside. He sat in front of the door. Occasionally, he'd look behind him and come eye-to-eye with Hatice's mother. He wanted to accompany Munise's tears but he refrained from crying. Rather than dealing with questions such as "Hey, what's it to you anyway?" he put up with gave into gulping bitterly. He turned around once more. His mother and Sevgi were holding a weeping Leyla's hand, consoling her. He couldn't see Munise. Upon tilting his head a little further inside, he saw Munise get up to take the Quran off the wall. Munise sighed inwardly, turned around and sat in her place. She removed the cover of the Quran, folded it and placed it on her knees. She did whatever she did in times when she wanted to read the Quran to take some peace of mind. It was one of prayers she constantly had in her mind to benefit from the word of Allah. She said "Fate" and opened to a random page. 'Fate' was none other than the sura she read on her first night in Istanbul.

"When the sun halts in its path,

the stars become fuzzy and go out,

and the mountains move."

When pregnant camels are set free

When wildlife is gathered up

When the seas boil over

When souls are matched with bodies

When it's asked what sins a girl committed to bury her alive…"

She was out of breath at this verse and could only say, "Sewi e mın." Only Leyla understood when she moaned saying "Oh my orphan." Munise became decrepit. She left the Quran in her lap so it wouldn't fall to the floor if she fainted. The fire flaring up inside her took on an unbearable state, and her head that grew heavy with the heartbreak of Hatice and her body that grew weak collapsed to her right side. Emine lifted up her heavy head. Her looks met with Leyla's eyes that turned bloodshot from crying, as she tried to complete the sura she'd memorized in her comatose state.

"When the labor registries have been opened

When the heavens have broke away from the ground

When Hell is ablaze

When Paradise is approached

Everyone is going to know what is to be prepared beforehand for that journey"

By now, Munise's energy had run down. She felt dizzy. Her head she could no longer hold up fell onto Emine's knees.

While turning his key around in the lock, Yılmaz also kicked the door with his foot. He charged angrily inside and picked up a plastic stool from the livingroom. Sauntering into the toilet, he placed the stool over the hole of the squat-style fixture. Out of breath, he stood up on it and tried to open a half-meter square small window overlooking the pitch-dark ventilation space. He was getting nowhere fast so he broke the window with his wrist. Though he was on the verge of losing self-control, he still was able to keep a cool head by not smashing his fist into the window. His hands needed him rock-steady. He reached his hand into the space that opened out. He wandered his hand over the wall. Taking care of the broken glass, he reached out a bit further and caught onto a rope he was looking for. He began winding the rope around his hand. The day he moved into the flat, he hammered a concrete nail into the ventilation wall, tied a blue laundry line purchased from the corner store to the nail and released it into the dark void. There was a black bag at the end of the line. The bag contained a Kalashnikov rifle he ripped off from the organization while he was in Diyarbakir and brought it to Istanbul to be used on such a day as today.

Breaking off the few pieces of glass of what was once the window, he brought the bag holding the Kalashnikov inside. He leapt off the stool and opened the bag's zipper at a stroke in the middle of the bathroom. With Abdurrahman's curiously looking on, he first opened the two layers of fabric, followed by five layers of thick plastic wrapping. He removed the Kalashnikov, holding it from its wooden rifle butt. He fumbled around the bottom of the bag, pulled out a full ammo clip and loaded it into the Kalashnikov. Then he placed the weapon he gripped tightly with his right hand back into the bag. Getting to his feet, he removed the 14-shooter handgun from his hip and handed it to Abdurrahman. He whispered growlingly, 'C'mon, we're outta here!"

They headed out the building without closing the door behind them and double-timed it from the dimly-lit street over to the avenue. In that short distance, Yılmaz told

Abdurrahman how he tossed Hatice's life in front of those shady characters while trying to save someone else's life. He gave another promise that he was going to nab Hatice from those fucking bastards. They flagged down a cab as soon as they reached the street. The tense expression on their faces not to mention the black bag in Yılmaz's lap bothered the cab driver. Were they coming from or going to a murder, were they coming from or going to a robbery? He couldn't figure out where they were coming from or where they were going. He deeply regretted picking up this weird fare. Just before they were to enter the highway, Yılmaz said, "Hey stop here," as he jumped out without leaving the bag in the cab, went over to the telephone booth on the sidewalk, giving the uni-eyebrowed cabbie, even more reason to get suspicious. He cocked an ear towards Yılmaz's conversation, made possible when he left both the cab door and telephone booth open. He overhead, "Hey, just get ready, we're going tonight, but we've got one last job to do." The clatter of a passing minibus prevented him from hearing the last part of his conversation. He was barely able to make out one more sentence like, ""Bring Doğan with you, Ferhat." Who were these guys Doğan and Ferhat?

"These guys are either gonna raid some joint or else kill someone!" His foot began trembling on the brake pedal out of anxiety. He raised his right hand to his thick eyebrows below his exposed forehead and began plucking them one-by-one as he did whenever he was in dire straits. His left hand reached down to his door pocket without tipping off

Abdurrahman. Groping around for the knife he kept stashed under a cleaning rag, he knew he needed to be ready for anything. He began praying he'd be able to drop these two guys off in Aksaray and hightail it out of there without getting in any trouble.

Yılmaz jumped back in the cab wearing a content expression on his face from taking care of an important matter. As the taxi headed back into traffic, the cabbie's right hand was still pressed up against his eyebrows. With Yılmaz in the front and Abdurrahman in the back, nobody uttered a single word until they arrived in Aksaray. They listened to the sound of their breath emanating from their lungs. Their airy beat was punctuated when Yılmaz said, "Stop." They had arrived in front of the nightclub. The cabbie slammed on the brakes in fear. Yılmaz, who most probably never wore a seatbelt in his life, nearly had his head go through the windshield. His left hand gripped the dashboard at the last millisecond. He shot the cabbie a stern look the moment he regained his wits, but didn't say anything. Quickly taking some money from his pocket, he handed it to the driver and got out of the cab without waiting for his change. Abdurrahman also leapt from the back. The cabbie stepped on the gas and turned into a side street without glancing at the money. Before the taxi's exhaust vapors had dissipated, Yılmaz and Abdurrahman bounded down the dimly-lit steps and headed straight into the tavern in the basement. The moment they entered through the door, Yılmaz came face-to-face with the frail waiter. He dived inside before the waiter had a chance to say, "Welcome sir." It was nearly four in the morning and the tavern was practically deserted. Drinkers had already done their drinking, those going were gone, and the bargaining to conclude the night in surrounding hotels had been conducted long ago. Only a few tables around the baseboards were full. The final conversations were held, the last chuckles were heard. Yılmaz came over to a table where a bald man and a hostess with big tits were gulping beer. He dropped the weapon bag in his hand in the middle of the table. In quickly opening the zipper and taking out the Kalashnikov, the playboy with no hair on his crown and the hostess with big tits froze where they were. Right behind them, the frail water halted in his tracks. The overpowering voice of the overture woman on stage and the dim lighting of the tavern had protected the distressed and womanizing state of affairs. They noticed neither Yılmaz nor his Kalashnikov. As it was, Abdurrahman was an ineffectual loser as usual. Despite the 14-shooter in his hand.

Kalashnikov bullets firing in quick succession into the ceiling turned the tavern into a state of pandemonium. The dim light bulbs shattered as they flew around. Pieces breaking away from the disco ball suspended from the ceiling extinguished the multicolored lights, as it spun and crashed to the dirty floor. The middle of the tavern was plunged into utter darkness as the weak lights illuminating the wall corners began to vibrate tremendously from the roar emanating from the Kalashnikov. Scared out of their wits, everyone was ranting and raving, crushing each other in a mad rush to hide under the tables. By now, everyone had their eyes on Yılmaz, who had his eyes on the management office door… He kicked in the door and dove in before those in the office had a chance to say, "What the fuck?" Everyone he sought was around a table full of glasses of arrack and fruit platters. The old single-toothed bastard was sitting in the boss's chair. The redneck with the crooked nose was in the armchair in front of the table and the burly rascal was facing him. Their faces were ashen and were all breathless when they saw the Kalashnikov. They didn't even wiggle their hands an inch in order to remove their guns on their hips. Even if they drew their guns at cowboy speed, they didn't dare challenge the Kalashnikov as they knew they'd be mowed down before they could pull the trigger. Lapsing into the armchair where he sat, the old man with the single tooth was on the verge of sliding under the table. But Yılmaz wasn't looking at this trio, but rather was shocked to see Leyla there, sitting fearlessly at the arrack table in the management office... She was simply sitting there in the chair next to the old man with the single tooth. Yılmaz looked like he had been hit in the brain with one of those bullets he just fired. I rescued you from this swamp just a few days ago. I had ripped your 15-year old body from the bosom of white-haired bastards at the risk of Pimp Ferhat's life, to boot…

- What are you doing here, Leyla? Did these bastards kidnap you?

- No, bro, I came here on my own.

- What are you saying, Leyla? What are you saying?

- What can I say, bro, they threw me outta the orphanage. Tell me, bro, what was I supposed to do? Where was I supposed to go?

- I'd be better for you to sleep on the street than to come back here, dammit!

- Forgetaboutit, do you think they'd let me sleep on the street by myself? I'd at least earn some money here rather than lie on an empty stomach beneath some penniless punks on the street.

- Shame on you, Leyla! Shame on you...

- Actually, bro, it's shame on Hatice.

Abdurrahman went bonkers when he heard his sister's name as he leapt from behind Yılmaz. He pointed his weapon at the old asshole with the single tooth, taking two steps and shouting: "Where's my Hatice, you mother fucking bastards? Then he turned to Yılmaz and asked, "Bro, you put my sister's life at risk for this whore?" Leyla's fearless eyes couldn't bear these words as she began sobbing. "I'm not a whore…" How was Leyla supposed to tell them what had befallen her the night Yılmaz left her at the orphanage?… How was she supposed to tell them that the night guard there pulled her small body under the stairs, clamped her mouth shut with one hand while bruising her breasts with the other hand, saying, "Are you always going to give it to others, you fucking slut?" What words could she have expressed to describe the teeth marks the guard with the onion-smelling breath left on her neck? Was she going to say, "I was going to be raped right there if someone upstairs hadn't turned on the stairway light?" Which sentences could she have fit all the words that described freeing herself from the clutches of the panicking guard, then ending up clinging to the arms of the redneck with the crooked nose after flinging herself back into the street, who then tossed her intp the back of the white Tempra without being able to wipe away her tears, only to be brought back to this swamp, where she was sitting with the threats of the old, single-toothed bastard next to her? How many breaths of life would she have left had she uttered that moment how the old, single-toothed bastard shouted, "Run away from me again and I'll kill both you and this girl," pointing to Hatice? Putting that all aside, what if she yelled at Yılmaz, "Hey stupid, why didn't it ever dawn on you the dishwashers were going to rat on you?" how many other people other than those in this management office were going to wander of the shores of death? She couldn't say any of this. She couldn't ask to account for a lifetime of troubles she experienced over the past couple of days. She couldn't rant or rave at the tavern rednecks who took their turns on top of her until the morning, or at Yılmaz, who wasn't capable of doing anyone a proper favor, or anyone else for that matter. She blustered at Abdurrahman. His evil words had burned her up inside so much that shooting her full of holes with the Kalashnikov in Yılmaz's hand wouldn't have caused as much suffering. "I'm not a whore, I'm not a whore…"

Leyla's tears were dripping onto her chartreuse dress and her leg that surged from her slit as she wept, leaning forward in her chair. She reacted by sobbing, "I'm not a whore," while squeezing her head with her two hands in vice-like fashion. The redneck with the crooked nose grinned wolfishly at Leyla's reaction. Noticing the looks of the redneck with the crooked nose, Abdurrahman went ballistic. Aiming his weapon at the old single-toothed bastard, he gripped the handle with the intent of a hammer, Although it was the first time he held a weapon, he managed this tough movement quite deftly. Flying from his place, he launched himself over to the guy with the crooked nose sitting in the armchair in front of him, shrieking, "Whadya grinning at, you SOB? Where's my sister, bitch, where's my sister?" the redneck's crooked nose was steeped in blood as he straightened up. Blood was spurting from a hole in his neck. After flattening the redneck's crooked nose, he meant to grip his weapon but unintentionally pulled the trigger as well. Abdurrahman lost all self-control when he saw the blood. He swung around and turned his gun on the burly rascal sitting in another armchair in front of the table. His eyes leaping from their sockets, the burly rascal reached for his waist. Just then, the office burbed with the sound of bullets. Yılmaz mowed down the burly rascal, who dared to shoot his cousin, in such a rain of bullets there wasn't a piece of him left between his neck and belly any longer than an inch.

Having a hard time coping with the violence, a trembling Abdurrahman dropped his gun to the ground. It was as if it wasn't him who had just jumped on top of the redneck with the crooked nose. On the contrary, Yılmaz had been more serene and decisive since the moment they entered the tavern. He intended to mow everyone down in the tavern until he took Hatice and pick off the rest once he got her all the way until he ran out of ammo. With the exception of Leyla of course… She was still a kid. She had a nice name. She was as beautiful as not to not dirty her hostess dress with the things she'd gone through…Turning the Kalashnikov barrel towards the old single-toothed bastard, he took a few steps towards the other side of the table. He took Leyla by the arm, lifted her up, and after shoving her over to Abdurrahman, towered over the old single-toothed bastard. He then planted the barrel of the Kalashnikov onto the old bastard's forehead.

- Where's Hatice, you old fuck, I'm not going to ask again!

- Wait a sec, bro, I'll be your bitch, please. Don't shoot, I'm beggin' you.

- You shithead! You either tell me, or you're through … You don't tell me and I'll plug you full of holes!

Slunk down in his armchair, the old single-toothed bastard continued pleading with the hope his life would be spared. He knew damn well that Yılmaz wouldn't kill him as long as he didn't give him Hatice. He also hoped one of the waiters inside had called his brother who ran a kebab shop in Bakırköy and was involved in the check mafia. He was trying to buy time until his brother and his armed men who hung around him like loyal dogs got here. With the worry that a day might come when he got into some hot water, Yılmaz researched and learned about all the venues he entered, as well as their owners, their owners' wives, friends and relatives. He knew that the old, single-toothed bastard was supported by a brother who was involved in the check mafia and didn't stay out of trouble in order to reinforce his reputation as a mafioso. He knew he'd be crashing his way into the tavern any minute now… For that reason, he had to move fast. As it was, there were already two dead bodies. The old single-toothed bastard needed to suffer pain in order to get him to talk. He pulled the trigger. He was going to send a bullet to his leg, but he didn't want to deal with adjust the Kalashnikov from rapid to single fire. The old single-toothed bastard held his disintegrating leg as he began to holler in agony.

- Tell me, fucker, tell me! Where's Hatice? Tel me, you son of a bitch!

- Bro, let me eat your shit, wait. Wait, enough, please. Fine, the girl's inside, in the scullery.

- You better be telling the truth, you fuckin' asshole!

- I swear to high hell, she's in the scullery, bro. I didn't do anything to the girl, bro.

- You better not have laid a hand on Hatice, You better not have laid a hand on her! I'll break off your flesh with a nail clipper, you fuck.

- Man, if I'm lying, they can fuck my family… I swear the girl's in the scullery, lemme be your bitch, just take the girl and go.

Yılmaz didn't trust the old, single-toothed bastard. Grabbing him by the collar with his left hand, he lifted him to his feet. Unable to remain erect, the old bastard shrieked as he crumpled to the floor. Yılmaz backed off the old bastard and gripped Leyla's arm. While he yanked Leyla out of the office, he turned to Abdurrahman. "Take that bastard and get behind me!"

Abdurrahman picked up the gun he'd dropped on the ground and hooked it on his waist. He grabbed the old bastard sprawled out behind the table and began dragging him by the arms. Because he was a regular there, Yılmaz was familiar with every corner of the tavern. He exited the office and turned right without entering the section where the tables were. He passed the restrooms, took a few more steps and entered the scullery. The tap was flowing full blast. Soapsuds overflowing from the dishwashing sink were floating on top of the water flowing from the rinsing sink. They were snowy white over a watery background.

The only sound coming from inside was that of the open faucet. It was clear the dishwashers fled into the garden the moment they heard the sound of bullets flying. Actually, Yılmaz was going to shoot the dishwashers in the mouth the moment he entered the scullery. He was going to mete out their punishment for ratting. He was forced to postpone this, saying, "You better believe I'll nail you sooner or later, mother fuckers." As it was, he forgot the dishwashers once Abdurahman entered the scullery dragging the old bastard.

Blood dripping from the old single-toothed bastard's shattered calf began dyeing the soapsuds red. Floating towards the drain at the foot of the door opening into the garden advanced as red and white twirls. Yılmaz swung a hard kick into the face of the old bastard, writhing in agony in the soapsuds. Crimson soadsuds gushing from the floor stuck onto Abdurrahman's face. A swath of the soapsuds flying through the air landed on Leyla's chartreuse dress, who was leaning against the scullery door as she wept. The single tooth on the old bastard's upper palate flew up with the blow of his kick to draw an upwards curve then falling into the rinse sink. The bloody tooth became shiny as it sank towards the bottom. The old bastard's two hands were also bloody. One was holding his trashed chin while the other one was holding his shattered leg. He couldn't speak because he couldn't move his mouth, but was able to grunt from his blood-filled throat… The grunting stopped once Yılmaz stepped on his throat with his foot. Pressing down hard on his throat with his wet, leather-soled shoe, he was on the verge of perishing the moment Yılmaz screamed, "Where is she, you goddamn pimp, where's the girl?" He raised his left hand for dear life and pointed to a large dirty white cabinet to Yılmaz' right side where the dishes were dried after washing and rinsing.

The shelves of the 1.5 x 2 m. cabinet were filled with plates. Right next to and above it, dirty dishes were stacked atop one another. Beneath this was a one-meter high cabinet where detergents, sponges and other sundries were kept on covered shelves. The two cabinets intersected at the baseboard. There was a rectangular space at the intersection point that wasn't noticeable at first glance when looking from the opposite side. Yılmaz turned slightly towards his right rear. Spotting the shelves full of dishes, he slammed his leather-soled shoe down on the old bastard's throat once again. He was pressing down with such resentment that his hard cornered heel pierced the old bastard's larynx. The old bastard had no intention of dying just yet. He persistently kept his left hand in the air, showing the dish cabinet with his pointer. Yılmaz slowly lifted his foot off the old bastard's throat, shouting, "If you're bullshitting me, then I'm just gonna have to line up your family right here and shoot them full of holes." The old bastard began grunting again. Yılmaz hurriedly turned around and went next to the cabinets. "What the fuck's here, goddamnit?" The Kalashnikov disintegrated the dishes on the shelves. Opening the covers of the small cabinet, he pushed the detergents, sponges, black trash bags and the sink pump into the soapsuds with the barrel of the Kalashnikov. Getting up in exasperation, he threw his finger on the trigger and was about to shoot up the old bastard's other leg when he noticed the gap in the corner. He reached out his head and looked into the space. Hatice was there, her hands, feet, mouth and eyes were bound… Her head tilted forward, she was wedged in that gap, in a knelt down position.

- Hatice! I'm here sweetheart, don't be afraid, here I am.

Slinging the Kalashnikov around his neck, Yılmaz lunged to extract Hatice from the gap. Grabbing her by the shoulders, he pulled Hatice upwards, over towards the cabinet where the dirty dishes were arranged. Hatice was whimpering like a kitten. Even the water flowing from the tap drowned out her moaning. Hatice's whimpering stoked Yılmaz's anger. He was on the verge of crying, but he had to remain steadfast. He also needed to hurry. The kebab shop mafioso might come barging in any second now. Without wasting time, he sat Hatice on top of the cabinet. He had just untied the knot of the black rag covering Hatice's eyes when he cringed at the sound of six shots fired in quick succession. Assuming the kebab shop mafia don had arrived, he unslung the Kalashnikov from around his neck and saw Abdurrahman's expressionless face as he turned. Seeing Hatice in her state, Abdurrahman drove three bullets right into the head of the old bastard, two to his forehead, one in the exact middle of his mouth… There were no longer any white soapsuds on the floor of the scullery as the entire place was painted red with the blood spurting from the old bastard.

Surprised that Abdurrahman killed the guy so easily, Yılmaz quickly regained his wits. They'd lost too much time as it was. He launched a mouthful of spittle towards the old bastard's head, which had turned into a bowling ball with bullet holes. He turned to Hatice no sooner as fast as his spit mixed in the blood. In a flash, he loosened the binds around the forlorn girl's mouth and eyes, then released her hands tied around her back. He hugged Hatice, as she began breathing regularly, crying out loud as her tears fell on the hair covering his neck. Meanwhile, Abdurrahman had released her legs from bondage. He began kissing his sister's feet, saying, "Dark girl." Scared stiff, Hatice was weeping in shock. Stooped over in that confined space for four and a half hours didn't resemble the corner she hid between her bed and wardrobe closet while the sound of gunfire came from outside during those dreadful nights in Silvan. While she felt a sense of security there, this space was no different from a tunnel of horror. She was screaming and wailing as she was taken out of the white Tempra and brought through the rear garden door. At that point, the overture singer on stage was swinging the microphone up and down as she strained her larynx in a lame effort keep in tune. Having almost faded out from all her clamoring, Hatice's voice didn't travel further than the scullery. Her bellowing was stifled completely when one of the young dishwashers was ordered by the old bastard to bind her hands and mouth with his soapy hands. Tying her hands and feet with the help of the other dishwasher, they then deftly shoved her into that corner gap, her heart nearly splitting in fear. She couldn't even scream out, "Mother." As it was during those interminable Silvan nights, she was always thinking of her mother. Was she still alive? Her mother's fluttering as she was being bundled into the white Tempra was still a vivid image in front of her eyes.

- How's mother, man….

- Mom's alright. Don't worry, everyone's fine, dark girl.

- I'm really scared, bro, let's go to mother's side, bro …

- Alright, dark girl, we're going.

- Man, who's the guy on the floor, is he dead? I'm really scared, bro.

- Don't look that way, dark girl, close your eyes, we're getting outta here.

Yılmaz bent over and picked up the roll of black trash bags he had seen in the cabinet a little while ago and scattered with the Kalashnikov barrel. Ripping off one of the bags from the roll, he placed the Kalashnikov into it then tapped Abdurrahman's shoulder, who continued to console Hatice. Tying a knot around the mouth of the bag, he handed it to Abdurrahman, then took Hatice in his arms. "C'mon, c'mon, get out the door…" Abdurrahman started walking towards the garden door. Yılmaz also took a few steps behind him. He was in a hurry, but he suddenly turned and looked behind him.

- Get moving Leyla, whadya waiting for over there?

- Let me be, man, this is my fate. Go and get Hatice. I'm done for anyway.

- Leyla, I'm telling you, get a move on. They're not going to let you live very long, so move it…

- Where to, man? I've got nowhere to go. You guys get outta here fast.

- Don't you have any place to go, dammit? I'll kill you, stick your body in a body and carry you outta here. I can't leave you here after all this, Leyla. So get your butt in gear.

Jumping over the old bastard lying on the floor, Leyla walked gingerly with her high-heels through the bloody soapsuds. The White complexion beneath her fishnet stockings were figured with blood stains. Realizing she would be unable to run comfortably, she left her high-heels at the bottom of the garden wall. Abdurrahman was on top of the wall. He first hoisted Hatice up and lowered her into the adjacent yard, then it was Leyla's turn. They came eye-to-eye on top of the wall. Having shot two people in cold blood without even looking behind him, Abdurrahman was on the verge of breaking down as he felt pangs of regret. The anguished look in Leyla's swollen eyes impaled him like a lance. He said, "Forgive me." Leyla gave him a bitter smile.

- C'mon man, whadya waiting for? You keep waiting there like that and they'll nail us. Get that girl down from there now, dammit!

Speeding up the pace with Yılmaz's warning, Abdurrahman lowered Leyla into the adjacent garden, handed her the bag the bag on top of the Wall, then he and Yılmaz dropped simultaneously down into the garden.

- Which way bro?

- I know we're going to go into the street from the gap on the side.

- We're not going out that way this time, Leyla.

Yılmaz didn't prefer the way Pimp Ferhat took when he abducted Leyla. It would've been suicide to come out onto the street the tavern was located. This time, they needed to come out right onto the rear avenue. That was the plan. Yılmaz turned his back on the apartment building next to the tavern and advanced towards the garden door of the opposite apartment building. He forced the door handle, but it didn't open. He stretched over to Abdurrahman's waist and pulled out his gun. He shot the glass out and handed the gun to back to Abdurrahman. He reached his hand in and opened the door. It was pitch dark inside as he pulled out a lighter from his pocket and lit it. They advanced with Yılmaz in front and Abdurrahman taking up the rear. After climbing a flight of stairs that appeared in front of them, they reached the main door of the apartment that opened onto the avenue. Tossing the lighter back in his pocket, Yılmaz poked his head out the door. He saw a green FIAT Doğan SLX parked right in front of the sidewalk. Having kept an eye on the apartment door for nearly an hour, Pimp Ferhat turned the ignition once he saw Yılmaz's face pop out. He lowered the automatic window glass and gestured to Yılmaz and those behind him. Yılmaz had a grin on his face as he whispered, "Hurry up." He bounded out ot the sidewalk in two step and opened the rear door of the Doğan. He closed the door once Hatice, Leyla and Abdurrahman had gotten in. Then he jumped in front. Pimp Ferhat stepped on the gas before Yılmaz shut his door.

03:45 AM

-Help! Thief! Catch that bastard! Thief!

I was still at the same spot, lying my semi-comatose state on the same concrete in front of the same store. My right arm pillowed my head, and had stretched my left arm over the coldness of the concrete. I suddenly felt excruciating pain in my left wrist. Opening my eyes, I saw some shoe treads. Someone had stepped on my wrist while running. He kept running without even turning around and apologizing. I understood when I began to hear more clearly voices in the distance. The punk who stepped on my wrist was a robber sprinting away like a jack rabbit. A few people passed in front of me in hot pursuit, shouting "Catch him, he's a thief." I also wanted to go after this thief. Of course, I couldn't do that. Although I had regained my awareness to an extent, I still hadn't the strength to get to my feet.

Seeing that I couldn't join the chase, I threw some choice expletives his way. And not because he treaded on my wrist, but just because he was a thief. I always thought all the evil in this world was fed with larceny. I couldn't go back on this thinking even in my inebriated state. Those who tell lies steal from the truth, those who rape steal from chastity, those who kill steal from life... Mother fuckers steal for the fuck of it. These lowlifes would steal the crusty underwear off you if they found the chance... I guess I exaggerated, do you think underwear is worth stealing? Dude, didn't they steal Dark Nuriye's underwear once?

It must have been early-November in 1995. Instead of sweating it up in the livingroom in front of a blazing stove, I was leaning against the wall of the icy-cold kitchen, munching on an apple. My mother was next to the washing machine, her hands and face ruddy from the cold. After filling the blue laundry basket with whites, she passed in front of me and went out onto the balcony. From the gap in the door, I watched as my mother began hanging the laundry on the line. She'd start murmuring one of her favorite folk songs whenever she undertook a chore. After hanging out garments like towels, shirts and trousers on the front line, she'd pin up the underwear one at a time on the rear clothesline. My mother would always hide our private garments. We heard the voice of our neighbor Nuriye coming from the balcony next door just as the last undershirt in the basket was being hung on the line. Looks like she was too late this time. She was a woman who spent her entire life on the balcony, who'd throw at least instigations at the heads of whomever she'd see in the surrounding windows, who'd give directions to passersby, and intrude if a dog urinated in the middle of the street by flying down from her balcony and landing on shit. Her face was also coal-black. I mean, her inside and outside were one and the same. It was for this reason, she earned a reputation in the neighborhood as 'Dark Nuriye.' She had nine kids, seven girls and two boys. The nine of them were like the leaves of parsley dipped in shit. It was obvious Dark Nuriye was going to stick her hooks into my mother, who hated this woman. She'd shake her head at her greeting, say 'yeah' at her gossip and just let her be. She pretended she didn't hear Dark Nuriye again. But she was quite persistent. She didn't quit calling out to my mother. I decided to perk up my ears this time. Apparently, someone stole the underwear she hung on her terrace. Just when I thought to myself, "Now what would anyone want with your underwear, you black-faced bat," Dark Nuriye announced what a stupid thing the thieves had done in her rude voice. The kids' underwear was stolen, nine pairs of them, to be exact. Dude, you don't mean to tell me this woman's nine kids wander about without underwear when they're being washed! Maybe there were a spare nine pairs of underwear lying about, but I was of the opinion those kids, aged six to sixteen, were wandering about without underwear when the faces of those kids passed in front of my eyes. It could be their indecency came from being without underwear. Of course, there was a stronger possibility it was passed down from their mother's nastiness, which was the reason the street

treated them with the consistency of dishwater. Anyways …
Dark Nuriye finally managed to reel in my mother. She was
talking about the underwear as if it were nine thick gold
bracelets that were stolen. Just as my mother had forgotten
the person facing her was Dark Nuriye, who was shorn of all
logic, she hit upon the brilliant suggestion, "Maybe they flew
off in the wind, maybe you didn't peg them to the line." And
of course, Dark Nuriye smacked the painful truth into my
mother's face once more. "My God, Emine, why would they
fly off in the wind, all that underwear was white. Lemme tell
ya, they were stolen by punk kids whose butts hadn't seen
anything but green underwear."

Thus, we learned then from Nuriye that wearing white
underwear was considered a status symbol. Concerned Dark
Nuriye's irrationality had been awakened from its dormant
state, Mother didn't feel like extrapolating this conversation
any further. After pegging a second clothespin onto the
undershirt, she picked up her basket off the floor and started
off towards the kitchen. One would think Dark Nuriye's
seditious brouhaha would cease and desist, but that just
wasn't the case. She began running off at the mouth. "Just
you wait and see if these thieving ways continue when one of
our guys comes into power." It was these words that stopped
mother in her tracks. She was thoroughly fed up with Dark
Nuriye bringing up politics every time they met. While
mother was a supporter of the party whose logo was "Let's
go further Turkey," my father loved the party that said, "We
can solve this business." Although they supported different

parties, they still loved each other very much. Dark Nuriye was pursuing the party that was on the rise after emerging first in last year's local elections. There was also the deputy election in late-December. Dark Nuriye staked a claim to the party she chased after like her son. She referred to the party directors as "our guys." Actually, she was right to identify so closely to her party. If we didn't count the handful of money she was paid in a month to sew party flags to be hung up in the streets, money she spent on a living room ensemble that was more expensive than the one we could barely afford over a year – she deserved this office of appropriation with the changes of the past year. She suddenly removed her surcoat and started wearing the burqa. Dark Nuriye had gone from someone who once took pleasure from hanging her boobs over the balcony bars and sniping, making impudent comments and laughing crisply at passersby, to someone who didn't leave her house without donning a burqa and black gloves.

Dark Nuriye was no exception, as practically all the neighborhood women kept abreast of this unstoppable trend. Always the ribald sort, Infidel Makbule didn't beat around the bush to join their midst. In fact, even aunts who'd been wearing burqas for as long as I've known were awestruck watching their neighbors, who chided them for years to the tune of "cockroaches" change their attire in no time flat. But for me, the biggest shock occurred with Dark Nuriye's tenant, Milky Way Aysel. She was a short, buxom woman in her '30s who was slightly flirtatious. She'd constantly chew gum, was chatty and mirthful to boot. We'd grumble to our mothers, but we'd get excited wondering which one of us Milky Way Aysel would send to the corner market whenever she came onto her balcony. In bringing her order, we'd run to and fro the corner store at warp speed hoping she calls us up to her place instead of her coming down to the apartment door. Fine, she was short, a bit on the chunky side, had a crooked nose, but I'd fulfill her market order by shopping at a store five districts away just to get an eyeful as she swung her hips, walking like a samba dancer at the Brazilian Carnival.

As a matter of fact, we had some wild booty hang-ups back then. This was the crime of Ali Şen, in particular, who got his team Fenerbahçe Brazilian vaccinations as soon as he was selected Chairman. As if the samba player transfer wasn't enough, he took the entire team to Brazil for pre-season camp. They held a banquet dinner there, which caused us to talk about Brazilian dancers, masters of shaking their booties, rather than Carlos Alberto Parreira, whose Brazilian National Team had won the World's Cup the previous year. The stately dancing women with their flawless bodies and long feathers attached to their headgear were etched into the center of our adolescent awareness. We watched the cheeky facial expressions of our soccer players on sports magazine programs here while dancers with dark complexions shook their dangling booties and nipples covered up with shiny glitter stars to undulating rhythms. The career success of those soccer players who warmed up in the erotic Brazilian climate was perhaps winding up the season with a championship after the preseason camp replete with booty tremors. Of course they got all wrapped up in soccer upon their return and were saved from a fleshy demise, but it was we who paid the price. We were struck by Milky Way Aysel's booty.

However, I was luckier than the other kids. Not compromising her witchy landlady attitude, Dark Nuriye didn't allow Milky Way Aysel use the terrace to wash her carpet, which led Milky Way Aysel to ring our doorbell. She asked mother if she could use our terrace to wash her carpet. Mother said okay, and I was assigned the hard work. I went and got Milky Way Aysel's carpet from her flat on the second floor and came down to the street. I leaned the carpet against our building's outer door to catch my breath. Then, I hoisted the carpet onto my shoulder and climbed three floors of steep stairs to emerge onto the terrace in a sweaty mess. Milky Way Aysel was right behind me. After leaving the carpet on the terrace, I turned around to go downstairs. Aysel's chomping on a piece of gum and she blurts out, "Wait, you can help me while I lift the carpet." I was blessed with something more than I hoped for. Who knows what circumstances I was going to find myself with Milky Way Aysel. Gasping for breath, I couldn't say anything, but shook my head in approval. I then placed two bricks on top of each that were sitting in the corner of the door and promptly sat on them and began watching Milky Way Aysel. She spread the carpet out on the terrace and attached the green hose to the water tap. She thoroughly soaked the navy-blue carpet with a huge red rose in the center. Because the water line on our terrace was not illegal, she shut off the tap without wasting water. She squirted some detergent onto the carpet then picked up a brush. She then sat on the carpet and began scrubbing. It was as if the brush in her hand was scratching my insides rather than the carpet. Before she took a seat, she had wedged her skirt between her legs in such a way that she had panties fashioned from her skirt on top of lily white legs. Well, that was the day I named her 'Milky Way' Aysel.

While Milky Way Aysel washed her carpet, she used all the tricks in the book to arouse me. As though the flagrant display of her milky white legs wasn't enough, she'd smile coquettishly on occasion, yank down the wide collar of her combed cotton top and stick her boobs in my eyes. Had I dove into the soapsuds covering the dark-blue portion of the carpet and caressed her milky-white legs, I'm quite sure she would've signed. She achieved her goal as I was wickedly turned on. Nevertheless, I was forced to suffice with watching her legs glaring beneath the sun. Had her husband Metin heard I had fondled his wife's milky-white legs, he most definitely would've fired on me. Fearing Metin, I sat cross-legged on the bricks at the risk of hurting my ass. So Milky Way Aysel's appetite wouldn't be swollen after seeing the growth in my body…

I sort of realized the pitch darkness that descended the neighborly conversations on our street the day our Milky Way Aysel, who previously applied mascara and wore narrow skirts to display her tight buttocks, began wearing a burqa.

As it was, because she didn't abandon overcoat and didn't participate in the weekend chat sessions at the association, my mother was constantly being harrassed by the sister, auntie, grandma group that donned the burqa later on. The wife of Enver of Samsun, Sevgi was a target of this gang for the same reason. The incident that really ascerbated the tension as when my mother and Aunt Sevgi refused to accept the steel casserole pots without lids. Prior to the election, women of the party with the bedsheet emblem went door-to-door in our neighborhood handing out steel pots without lids in exchange for promises of votes. They weren't giving the pot lids in order to guarantee the promise of votes in their favor. Lids were going to reunite with their pots according to the results that emerged from the neighborhood ballot box during the final week of December. Besides mother and Aunt Sevgi, nobody else from our street refused the crockery. There were even those who took the non-lidded pots after fibbing they'd vote for the party on the rise. In fact, when she dropped by to drink tea, Milky Way Aysel said, "Emine, maybe you should have taken one of those pots. You would've received a lid had they won and if not, you could've rigged a lid on your own anyways." As usual, mother was ready with one of her replies of the sledgehammer to the brain provision in such situations: "One can't cook legitimate food in an illicit pot, my girl." After Milky Way Aysel received her lesson, she closed her booty which wanted to jump out from her skimpy skirt and went home.

My mother and Aunt Sevgi always remained resolute. Yet, the neighborhood peer pressure had been racheted so high that they succeeded in aggravating even my mother, who had adapted a life philosophy of not getting involved in business that didn't concern them in normal conditions. This is why she got angry at Dark Nuriye's words that began with the underwear thieves and wound up with politicians wearing ties with armchair cover ties. She put the laundry basket on the ground once more and extended her body from the balcony in order to get a better look at Dark Nuriye. "What, are you telling me the underwear thieves are going to be caught once your party comes to power?" From Dark Nuriye's wheezy, strained response I understood she wasn't used to mother's retorting like that. There was no holding back mother any longer when Nuriye said, "You better believe they'll be caught, our guys have plenty of influence." She was like a sidekick with a rapid fire reply. The stage was hers. "Don't trust those with too much influence, or else they'll steal your underwear and you'll be up shit's creek without a paddle, Nuriye!" Dark Nuriye finally met her match and kicked in the afterburners with a list of points she recalled from the conversations she listened to at the association. "My girl, our guys won't be raising a generation of thieves, they'll be raising Moslem kids. We watched a video at the association, I was amazed at what this guy said, 'I hadn't heard of or seen a father who learned thievery from his son.' Thievery passes from the father to the son, Emine. Our guys aren't going to raise thieving sons." It seemed as though Dark Nuriye was putting together logical sentences for the first time in recent memory. However, mother was ready to hit back with logic of her own showing she knew the true face of politicians and that she wasn't going to be fooled by their swagger… She gave Dark Nuriye a piece of her own bitter medicine, saying, "Forget about them for now, Nuriye, if Allah ordains it, we'll live and see for ourselves exactly who taught their kids what lessons." Dark Nuriye looked like a jigsaw puzzle with a couple of pieces gone.

Seeking revenge for the devastating pot shots she ingested, Nuriye started swinging fists of no predetermined destination. That's when I also stepped onto the balcony. I intended to bring mother, who had been exposed to enough of Dark Nuriye's harrassment, back inside before she suffered a nervous breakdown. I looked to see that Dark Nuriye was taking out pieces of red cloth from the sack on her balcony. She took one and showed my mother. It was the flag of the party on the rise. Its edges had yet to be sewn. She showed the emblem in the middle of the piece of fabric and said, "Look, this means abundance." She added, "It's because of you the country's got no abundance." Mother ignited her gunpowder.

- Nuriye, Can you hear what you're saying? Why is it because of us that there's no abundance in the country?

- Because you don't vote for Moslems, that's why! Moslems are with Moslems and infidels are with infidels.

- Nuriye, What, do you think you're all Allah now that you're wearing the burqa? Allah knows who's a Moslem, who's an infidel and who's a hypocrite.

- You just keep talking ... Look what happened in Antalya!

- What happened in Antalya?

- It was totally flooded.

- May Allah help them Nuriye. What can I do?

- Don't you get it, girl! They didn't vote for Moslems, and Allah damned them!

- Let Allah do what you know, Nuriye! People are free to vote for whomever they wish, that's Allah's disaster. It could happen to all of us.

- Look, do disasters hit cities where our guys have won? Let's face it, Allah is on the side of the Moslems.

- Are you telling me El Nunu happened because they didn't vote too? May Allah give you some brains, Nuriye, what else can I say?

Kudos for my smart mother! Dark Nuriye was dumbstruck when she mentioned 'El Nunu.' The El Nino hurricane hit America at the same time the flood disaster occurred in Antalya. Even though she incorrectly memorized the name, it was clear mother remembered it from the news. As she told off Dark Nuriye, it didn't really matter if she mispronounced the name of the storm. I wanted mother to quit while she was ahead, so I held her hand and said, "C'mon, let's go inside." Yet, Dark Nuriye was a few steps away from the slander summit. At any moment, she might have driven mother mad by blurting out, "Had the Americans voted for the party on the rise, they might not have been hit with El Nunu." Thank Allah mother believed that avoiding slanderous accusations was the most beneficial way as she gripped my hand tightly and followed me towards the kitchen. Closing the balcony door, she went into the bathroom to leave the basket in her hand, then she returned. Picking up the tray on the counter, she sat on the floor and began removing stones from the rice to cook for dinner. She was reticent as if the tension hadn't occured a few moments ago. This was a side of my mother I really appreciated. She never reflected unpleasant matters that occurred outside at home. She didn't even want the walls to hear. This is why for her, Dark Nuriye's evilness stayed on the balcony. Because I knew this trait of hers, I couldn't dare say, "Good for you, mother." I sat on the floor and leaned my back against the wall. While continuing to eat my apple I sliced with a bread knife, I watched her drag the grains of rice on the tray with her plump fingers. The sound of rice grains dragging on the tray in our ears as mother sifted through the rice like she was plucking the strings of a canon she sitting in her lap at the same tempo. The tune of the grains of rice sung in rhythm with the tray only suppressed my apple bites from time to time. We sat for awhile without talking, within a sense of calm until cleansing of the rice was finished. Our tranquility was ruined by some familiar voices coming from outside. Hastily leaving the tray in her lap on the floor, mother exclaimed, "What's going on?" She got to her feet and peered outside from beneath the curtain, then hurried over to the door, opened it and went onto the balcony. This time I immediately crept onto the balcony behind mother without waiting inside. I understood why mother reacted so quickly to the voices coming from outside. The owner of the voice that got mother to her feet belonged to our opposite neighbor, Aunt Sevgi. I was born and grew up on this street and this was the first time I heard Aunt Sevgi shouting. When Aunt Sevgi saw mother, she started to cry, "Emine, take a look at what she did to that kid." Crushed in the face of my mother, Nuriye the Witch took her revenge on Aunt Sevgi's little girl, Elif, who was playing hopscotch in the street with her peers. Dark Nuriye shouted from her balcony to the kids around Elif – two of whom were of her own making- "Don't play with her, why do you let infidel kids play with you?" Fearful of Dark Nuriye, the kids kicked Elif out of the game. Elif was bawling when she arrived home and when she told everything that happened, Aunt Sevgi was totally stunned, especially when she asked, "Mom, are you an infidel?" She got pissed off and came onto the balcony. The poor woman really took the discrimination her little girl was faced with to heart, and felt terribly hurt. It was obvious she tea shed tears when she said to Dark Nuriye, "Don't you have any fear of Allah? What could you possibly want from little kids?" Just then, I looked at Nuriye, and saw in her the epitome of the evil woman character roles of

Suzan Avcı. She had an expression on her face of disgusting pride that wasn't ashamed of the evil she committed. Aware of the evil she brought upon the little kid, she was quite pleased with the result. Aunt Sevgi reproached Dark Nuriye, "What have we ever done to you, Nuriye? You sound like a broken record, 'infidel, infidel… Excuse me, but who the hell do you think you are, Allah?" Dark Nuriye shriveled up her eyes and face and got herself worked up to get on her broomstick and fly off her balcony. I got it, Dark Nuriye wanted nothing more than to worry Aunt Sevgi to death. Consequently, in also damning my mother, she had the intention of hitting two birds with one stone. She knew quite well that the only neighbor on the street my mother liked was Aunt Sevgi. Which was why she didn't look my vociferous mother in the face and attacked Aunt Sevgi. Once again, she was enumerating the sentences in her memory.

- Moslems stand next to Moslems. Infidels are next to infidels. Look, your girl went back home bawling her eyes out.

On the verge of passing out, Aunt Sevgi grabbed onto the balcony windbreaker as she sat heavily where she was. She no longer was visible behind the balcony's solid steel plate and only sobbing was heard. Shaken with little Elif, Dark Nuriye had succeeded in destroying Aunt Sevgi with her elder daughter, Meryem. As the gaping wound of Aunt Sevgi's heart, Meryem was a smart girl, having finished high-school at valedictorian. We would always run to Meryem whenever we couldn't do our homework assignments. She'd help us do our homework without any hesitation and explain subjects we couldn't understand better than our teachers. In taking her brother Erkan's lead, she was the second person on the block to get into university. She was accepted into İstanbul University's Law Faculty, and her intention was to become a lawyer. She got ambushed in the pass. I remember the day she went to enroll on campus. She was really happy as she left the neighborhood in the morning. The Meryem I saw as she returned was in stark contrast with the Meryem I saw in the morning. Someone had stolen the happiness from her face. Her eyes were bloodshot. She was reprimanded by the student affairs office for showing up with her headscarf. They insulted Meryem and made her cry in front of classmates she had yet to meet. When in fact she also brought a photo of herself without a headscarf so she wouldn't get into any hot water during the enrollment process. But no sooner did she pass through the gate when officials there started bitching at her, "Take off your headscarf, you're at school, not at a mosque!" According to what Meryem told us, the matter that upset her the most about this denigration was that it was the women officers who were doing all the hassling.

Having gotten over the shock of enrollment day, Meryem sunk into the abyss of darkness once the scholastic year got underway. Each of the round blanks on the university entrance exam form Meryem filled in with a dull pencil had become a black hole that blackened her life. Meryem began to melt down as time passed. She was pensive, sad, and walked with her head bent down all the time. She was no longer participating in the courses she brown-nosed her way into at the start of the year. In fact, not only was she kept from entering the amphitheater, she and her head-scarf wearing friends weren't being allowed onto campus anymore. She'd sit in front of the gate with her head-scarved friends, then return home. Around that time, these sittings turned into a movement. It was a carnation movement that had began against the persuasion rooms set up at the campus entrance, against gates that were shut in the faces of those wearing head scarves, against the crushed efforts, against squashed rights, against the insults and belittling. They held carnations in their hands as they shouted in unison, "'We're going to succeed," when in fact, they weren't very hopeful. A melody had descended upon their lips…

"Don't cry carnation

Don't make me cry

Wipe your tears away"

While the elegant voice of the melody said, "don't cry carnation," they were crying non-stop and nobody was wiping their tears away. We were watching them on the nightly news, right after the 'shocking' images the famous correspondents caught by hunting down the middle-school students on their way to prayer services. I had also seen Meryem in their midst. They all had tears on their cheeks. It wasn't the fear of billyclubs about to throttle their bodies that made them cry. It had now become a habit of the police force to forcibly remove the headscarves off a few of the girls sitting in the front rows, and intimidate those in the back rows. They wanted to the pain they experienced to be increased exponentially. The fact that it was the women police officers yanking off their headscarves made the situation even more intriguing. That famous idiom, 'A scorpion wouldn't even be the cause the evil a woman can cause another woman' should have changed. Well, this unconscionable act that was the reason for the tears that ran down their naive cheeks. I was also crying as I watched them. I might not have cried had Meryem not been amongst them, but then again I'd have felt quite depressed. I never forgot how I cried while watching the news bulletin one night, thinking aloud, "Man, don't these police officers have any mothers or sisters of their own?" My father looked at me crossly and said, "Quit your sniveling, son, it's not Allah breathing down the police force necks, it's their commanders. One day, they'll beat up Muhammed, the next day, they'll beat Fidel." Then again, I thought of Meryem's plight and cried once more. What a pity, all that effort this angelic girl went through in the midst of depravity... It meant those who worshipped their commanders instead of Allah had no clue about pity...

While this tyranny had gotten me down alright, who knew what sort of wringers Meryem had been put through. As it was, she had thrown up a white flag when she abandoned her studies before the first semester was over. It was raining outside the day she made her final appearance at school. I had picked up a loaf of bread from the bakery and was on my way home. It was the first time I'd seen Meryem cry on our block. She had been crying out in front of the university, on the bus, in the park, here and there, but she poured her tears inwardly once she arrived on our block. I guess she didn't want the neighborhood women seeing her in that state in order not to be a party for the gossip windmill. I may have been the only one on our block who saw Meryem crying. She entered her home meekly, silently with carnations in her hand, her black bag on her back and a drenched headscarf and overcoat … I didn't see Meryem for a long time after that day, for almost three weeks, to be exact… I assumed she had gone to stay with relatives who lived near the university. I no longer saw her in the 'now time for the fundamentalism news' on the nightly news. It meant she was no longer going to school… So where was this girl? Aunt Sevgi provided the answer to this question when she popped on over for tea on a rainy night. Meryem had been holed up in her room just crying her head off for the past three weeks. We understood why Meryem had shut herself up in her room once Aunt Sevgi cried herself a river. When in fact, Meryem wasn't the kind of girl who would leave school and throw in the towel of life.

- Why did your girl just shut herself up in her room, Sevgi?

- Emine, if only you knew what happened to us…

- What happened girl, just let it out …

- Sister, well you know the damned authorities didn't allow these girls into class because their heads are covered…

- So what?

- They protested in front of the school for a few days … I don't know how many times I told her, look girl, forget it, don't go, their immorality has become chronic and won't look in your face. I told her so many times… She didn't listen, saying, "I'm going to study," and she went. What happened then? My child was beaten every day.

- What can I say, girl, May Allah damn them. The kid worked so hard, toiled, and won entrance to the university. Now they won't let her inside.

- Then again, none of this would've deterred Meryem… Look, I don't know how can I put it…

- Whadya mean, girl, did something worse happen?

- Yeah, you better believe it. Looks like there are some real sons of bitches out there.

- Whadya mean by that, girl?

- It means that there are atheists who act as though there is Allah.

- Whadya mean, girl, why don't you tell me in a way I'm going to understand.

- Emine, you know these girls organized a sit-in protest lin front of the school, well some guys began coming over to their side.

- Who are they?

- Just some rich guys. They went to the poor girl's side supposedly to give them support. Sometimes they'd bring food and drink, sometimes they'd stand beside them.

- So, what was the matter with that, girl?

- Wait a sec, sis, I'll tell you what the matter was with that? One of the guys put a move on our Meryem. He was short, fat, around 50 years old with a thin, twisted beard. He has a textile business in Merter or so he said… They also have a businessmen's association and he's supposedly the vice-chairman of that association. He always went by Meryem's side with the excuse of helping her. He was constantly being fresh with her, but she didn't respond in kind even though he was constantly pressuring her.

- What a scumbag!

- Wait, sister, there's more to the story… The day she came home crying was because this scumbag said some crap to Meryem. These girls gathered in front of the school, then they gathered at that scumbag's association that day. While Meryem sat with the other girls in the association hall, this scumbag went over next to her and said let's talk for a couple minutes, then called her into his room. Come and be my wife, we can have a religious engagement. I'll set you up in a home in Başakşehir, I'll give you a car, etc.etc.etc

- He proposed marriage to the girl without considering the age difference, the old geezer?

- What marriage, Emine, what marriage. Apparently, the guy was already married. The cuckold wanted my daughter for his second wife. I'll have you live like a queen, you can study at home, etc.etc.etc…

- What a douchebag scumball. The psycho was after a girl young enough to be his granddaughter?

- Yep, sister, and to think that Meryem hasn't come out of her room since then. My baby's been crying ever since "It wasn't those who didn't let me into the school it was some opportunist atheist who burned me out."

- May Allah damn them all. May Allah rain down grief and misery on those who prevented the miserable kids from studying at school and the bearded faithless who hindered their progress as well. May Allah rain down grief and misery. May Allah rain down grief and misery.

My mother pleaded three times in quick succession for Allah to rain down grief and misery upon the shameless schemers to make desperate girls their second wives. She continued to plead to Allah when she heard from Aunt Sevgi how many girls who left their homeland to study only to be deceived by such schemers. To an extent, she consoled

Aunt Sevgi when she said, "Allah took pity on you Sevgi, thank heavens he protected your daughter." It's true, he had rescued Meryem from the clutches of the wizened panderers at the price of her being weary of life. Dark Nuriye dished up the tyranny they were unable to unleash. Aunt Sevgi was crushed in the corner of the balcony by two poisonous sentences. Aunt Sevgi's sobbing had subsided by now and it was clear she had collapsed from exhaustion. Was she supposed to fight the university's repressive army, think about the wizened panderers who took advantage of the oppressed who were screwed over by cruelty, or else be patient with a neighbor whose heart was darker than all of them...

She prayed for a while, finishing her prayer by whispering, "Make me cry, make me laugh, revive me, kill me, this love is both a servant to you, your damnation is pleasant as is your courtesy." Meanwhile, Elif perched at her mother's side, and stretched out in her lap. Aunt Sevgi gradually came to her senses. Her eyes were constantly on her elder daughter Meryem. Her face smiled in an odd manner. I was sure she enjoyed the fact that Meryem had come out of her room. Considering the calm that spread from her smile, it's possible she was thankful for the bad moment that caused her to faint. Had she not experienced that moment and not lost consciousness, it was a strong possibility Meryem wouldn't have emerged from her room for many days to come.

- Girl, can you say that last prayer again.

- That wasn't a prayer, mother, that was a poem by the İbrahim Tennuri.

- İbrahim who?

- İbrahim Tennuri, mother. The poem leaves as much an impression as a prayer, doesn't it?

- You can say that again, girl… Go ahead and say that wonderful poem then

- "Make me cry, make me laugh, revive me, kill me, this love is both a servant to you, your damnation is pleasant as is your courtesy."

- That's it, girl, the damnation of the almighty is pleasant as is his courtesy.

Aunt Sevgi's state of mind was exactly as I thought. The well dug with Dark Nuriye's poisonous tongue and filled with the matter in breast was a provision for temporary misery for Aunt Sevgi. The blind well she had tumbled into was illuminated by her daughter's face and had turned into a rose garden. It was the reason for her to have Meryem repeat the poem she was hearing fort he first time. "Praise Allah, your damnation is pleasant is as well as your courtesy …"

Meryem never asked what had happened, or why her mother had passed out on the balcony. She knew that renewing the pain and suffering was nothing than a massacre of a smile. She smiled and hugged her mother as though it wasn't her that was struggling with very heavy burdens.

"Let me brew some tea, Aunt Emine" as she went into the kitchen. The tea pot I saw at the foot of the balcony door had become a good excuse for me to have a face-to-face talk with Meryem. I longed to have a conversation with her, I had missed the stories she told, the poems she read, her addressing kids as 'dude,' but the thing I missed the most was the smile on her face... I wondered why she was so down on herself. Fine, she put in a lot of effort but wasn't allowed into the school she had earned a right to attend and was subject to insults. That said, the Meryem I knew wasn't the kind of person who was about to throw in the towel of life. The moment I entered the kitchen with the empty teapot, I cut to the chase without any hesitation by asking Meryem, 'Why did you choose death?" She had stuck the small teapot under the tap and was cleaning out the morning tea. She looked in face, and didn't spare me one of her smiles I'd missed. She inhaled deeply and went quiet, remaining that way under the teapot was spic-and-span. Just then, mother called from inside, "You went to put some tea up, what have you been doing for the past two hours? Meryem come over here girl and let's take a look at you." Meryem didn't break her reticence, so I hollered to mother from the kitchen door that Meryem was washing the teapot and that we would be there in a bit. I then continued to watch Meryem. I waited patiently to speak as the Meryem I knew wasn't one to give up so easily. She had a tough makeup that wouldn't even give up on the street games we played when we were kids. She was always the winner with her smarts, her ambition and enthusiasm. For instance, I would always follow Meryem whenever we played hide-and-seek. Thanks to Meryem's smart maneuvers, she knew in which direction 'it' was going to look, and where 'it' was going to look for who where, we were never tagged. Great, so what was it that made you get tagged and leave the game, Meryem? Tokay I understand, that S.O.B. may have gotten to you but you were someone who could've stopped him in his tracks.

Maintaining her reticence, she ran the lid through the water then put the teapot on the counter. Motioning me to give her the large kettle, I took a few steps over to her. Handing her the kettle, I looked in her eyes and asked her once more. "Meryem, why did you choose death when there was a struggle path?"

- I didn't die, look, I'm right across from you.

- Cut it out, Meryem, even your mother missed your face. How many weeks have you been lying in a grave? Aunt Sevgi spends her entire day praying in front of your door like she was visiting a tomb, don't tell me you don't know that? The poor woman cries her eyes out every time she visits us.

- I know, honey, I know.

- Wonderful, if that's the case, then why did you have to go and upset your mother so much, Meryem? I know the troubles you've been through, but wasn't it you who said, solitude is persecution and despair is death? Tell me why you left life and chose death sis, why?

- No I didn't, honey. I could've found a shorter and less painful way if I wanted to die instead of living. I just copped out, that's all.

- From who?

- From evil people, honey. People like those who call me a fundamentalist and kick me out of school, or another who calls mother an infidel and makes her cry. They don't leave us alone to recite our 'Ya sin' prayers on Friday evening so we can sleep peacefully. They caused me so much pain that I fled all this hypocrisy so as to not kill myself, honey. I even emulated the cruel women at school and set myself up a persuasion room.

- Okay, but was it worth it? I mean, look at the shape your mother's in. Dark Nuriye said stupid shit about you that almost killed the poor woman.

- Don't you think I know that, honey! I had a good idea why my mother collapsed in the balcony corner like that. School's one thing, but we're really being tested with these instances. We can struggle against bans, no problem, but it's the women wearing burqas who sow dissension and malice and men who hide a mountain of evilness behind a wisp of beard who worry me. You have no right to state your point of view, they're Moslem, you're the infidel…

- Never mind, sis. Allah knows what's ticking inside of everyone. How about that, looks like you and I are the only ones left. I think it's best if we support each other.

- You're right, honey, you're right, how are they going to come clean in front of Allah with their so-called righteous dues?

- You can forget about all that as well, sis, at the rate we're going, we're going to have plenty of company in Hell. God forbid, but if we ever commit some evil doings, at least we feel out of place in the middle of the flames if we end up there.

- Yep, you're right, dude, even though they're not of high positions, we'll have company in Hell. Starting from right now.

04:03AM

-Are you ill man, what's the matter with you?

- It's nothing, I'm fine, man.

I'm fine, yeah right. Anyone lying down here at this hour is either drunk or else homeless. What the fuck kind of question was that anyway? I said the bit after "I'm fine" aloud as I couldn't open my eyes to get a bead on the guy who questioned my welfare. Nothing happened to me because once I said I was fine, the good-for-nothing cunt who posed the question was long gone. For fuck's sake, you'd assume the dude would wonder what someone saying he fine was doing sprawled out on the ground like that. But no, just a meaningless question, "Are you ill?", then take off like a hoser. As it was, taking off hoser-style was always the best way in dealing with the sort of standoffish questions that put me at ease, that make it clear that I give a shit but that I don't want to get involved with someone with problems... Didn't Ferda always used to do that as well?

After earning a spot in this city's prestigious mechanical engineering department, I was very pleased when I saw Ferda in my class. It was then when I felt proud of my success. After Hatice, it was the first time I'd encountered a girl who put a smile on my face. After my devastating experience with Hatice, I forgot about her and wasn't very hopeful on whether or not I was able to take another passionate plunge. Then again, I needed endearment that would make me forget about Hatice's departure. Ferda, who got me excited, could fit the bill quite nicely. Because there was a huge, bloody photograph that I needed to forget and Hatice was in that image.

I spent the night Hatice was abducted on the balcony. I waited until dawn for her cousin and brother to bring back my Hatice. She never came back. A taxi entered the block around the time I'd dozed off leaning my head on the balcony bars. It pulled over in front of Hatice's home. I looked at my watch and it was seven-thirty. I recognized the guy who got out of the cab as Hatice's uncle, the guy who rented the place. His head was leaning forward as he knocked on the door. The door opened on his first knock. Hatice's uncle entered without a word. The door remained open and five minutes hadn't passed when the previous night returned to Hatice's home in full regalia. Once again, Aunt Munise and Leyla's shrieks resounded around the block. What happened, did something dreadful happen to Hatice? I perked my ears up and tried listening in, but didn't understand anything as they spoke in Kurdish. Goddamn me for not knowing the language of the girl I loved. It wasn't long before Hatice's uncle got Aunt Munise to come outside and get into the cab. He went back inside and this time, he got Leyla outside and into the taxi as well. Both Aunt Munise and Leyla were shrieking at the top of their lungs. It was certain something terrible had happened to my Hatice. Man, if only I could understand what they were saying, but I couldn't, not even a single word. I got up to go downstairs, but I couldn't take a single step. Hatice's uncle got into the cab without even pulling the house door shut. They just took off and haven't been back ever since that day.

I learned what had transpired the following day. Newspapers had changed hands many times. Not just on our block, but throughout the entire neighborhood. I dropped by Latif's barbershop to have him spread some free brilliantine in my hair. I didn't want my Hatice to see me looking like a sleazebag when she returned. I still had my hopes. Latif was talking with a customer when I entered the shop, "Yeah, they lived right over there. It's a real shame what happened to them, look, it's all in the papers," as he reached out his hand holding a comb to the newspaper. Looking at the paper in his helper's hand, I grabbed it from him and looked at the huge headlines on page three, "Bloody execution on the shore road..." There was a huge photo beneath the headlines. A Doğan had gone onto the sidewalk and there were people inside with blood all over them, but their faces were blotted out so it wasn't clear who they were. I read the news inserted next to the photo. "There was a Mafia hit in Samatya. The shore road was turned into a bloodbath. According to information obtained, events unfolded thusly: Starting from Aksaray, a car carrying underworld mobster and Bakırköy kebab shop owner Sefer Karagül began following a car with five people in it, two of whom were minors. Once they reached Smatya, Sefer Karagül and his men cut off the car they were following, strafing it with bullets. Striking the sidewalk, those in the car fired back with a long-barrelled weapon. Those in the car that was shot up in the firefight died and were identified as; Yılmaz Çekiç (32), Ferhat Duygulu (30), Abdurrahman Çekiç (19), Hatice Çekiç (14) and Leyla Ağrılı (15). It was determined that of those who lost their lives, Abdurrahman Çekiç and Hatice Çekiç were siblings who were the cousins of Yılmaz Çekiç. Wounded in the battle, Sefer Karagül and two men were taken to a local hospital via an ambulance that arrived at the scene. Another man was taken into custody. The bodies of the five who died were taken to the mortuary. While the investigation regarding the incident is ongoing, it has been stated as a mafia payback."

I slumped down in one of the chairs lined up behind the barber's chair as I spread the paper on my knee. While looking at the section of the photo blotted out in grey, I added another 16 to my 16 years of age. I wonder which one of those behind this grayness that only reflected the color of blood, was my Hatice? I no longer worried about "what they were going to say" as I broke down in tears. I sobbed as if I had just lost my mother. Both Latif and his helper were asking why I was crying. I couldn't respond. I wiped my tears with my fingers that were smeared with newspaper ink. I lifted my head, looked in the mirror to notice I looked like a commando with underliner. The crying commando… Latif the barber just wouldn't shut up, saying, "What the fuck, I'd understand if they were relatives, but don't be so softhearted or else you'll get the shit kicked outta you in the army." Then it dawned on him, as he smirked, "Don't tell me you had a thing for that little girl, you little candy shop kid!" I couldn't decide whether I should get pissed off at what this smartass said, or take pity on his insensitivity. I got up and went into the street. Looking at Hatice's home with the door wide open, I contemplated going inside but I couldn't get up the nerve. My fear of "what would they say" reared back up and bit me in the ass, so I went home. I told my mother what had happened. She began weeping, as she cried, "Oh, I'm so sorry for their souls." I cried again once she started crying, Though I thought just how embarrassing it was for us to be crying, I still wept the entire day. Once the days I had mourned over Hatice's death had passed, I began to feel pangs of regret. If only I had gone into her home and taken a tiny souvenir the day I read that gloomy news. Once Munise didn't return, the German-Turkish landlord loaded all their possessions into a truck and sold them to a second-hand goods dealer. That action made me cry once more.

Ferda was a girl who was supposed to make me forget the huge scar inside of me. At least that's what I thought but it took me four years to realize I was mistaken. I did everything in order persuade the dimple-cheeked Ferda. I was always behind her like a backpack. I carried her Zero cola to her table in the canteen, I signed her name during roll-call, I gave her my lecture notes during finals, and began carrying the brand of cigarettes she smoked, as I didn't want her to be without cigarettes when her pack ran out, I consoled when she was sad, and wantd her to be happier when she was happy and there were even a few time when I skipped Friday prayers just so I could be at her side a little more, may Allah forgive me. Casting evrything aside, I really loved he. However, whenever I'd say, okay, this business is done, I'd receive a solid kick from Ferda. She was totally messing with my head. She'd laugh in my face, give me some sweet talk, hold my hand while we strolled about, get a kick out of strumming my fingers through her auburn hair, and put her head on my shoulders and close her eyes whenever we sat on a bench. If this wasn't love, then what was it for God's sake? It wasn't. If what you call love is one-sided, then it was an emotion that was apt to do something stupid. Actually, I should have understood when Ferda didn't carry these pleasant situations beyond campus, that her looks that gave me hope weren't to do with love at all. There was no going to the movies, no concerts… We didn't rendezvous outside, not even once. She didn't 'okay' to even my only offer. She didn't go on any school fieldtrips, and didn't participate in any summer festivals. She refused me every time I offered to leave her at home and obstructed me every time I went after her. Though I didn't deem it likely she was destitute and hiding at home like the poor girl – rich boy films, I always mulled over this possibility. Then again, I wasn't rich either. There was something else behind this, but what?

I'm not going to elaborate on the stuff that happened in the interim. As it was, it was mostly situations that ended in disappointment. In our senior class, I was forced to say "we're either finished or we continue." How was I going to see Ferda again once school finished? It was certain she wouldn't even attend the graduation ceremony, and she didn't. Thanks to my technical instructor, I found a trainee position that paid minimum wages with a firm in Levent. I wore my suit for the first three days of the week, I still don't know why trainees had to wear suits. I didn't drop by school on those days. In this situation, I only had two days of the week in which I could come side-by-side with Ferda and that was until the end of May. Then, it was going to be 'School's out, Ferda's gone." I was decisive about talking with Ferda and putting a name on what we had lived. Not to mention getting her to account for teasing me… This talk wasn't going to take place on campus because in order for me to confront the real Ferda, we needed to talk somewhere far from school grounds. I made this decision before I fell asleep on Sunday night.

In the morning, I put on my suit, shined up my leather-soled shoes with a shoe polish sponge, caught a bus and went to my trainee job. Until now, our class had as many as three laboratories. Before one in the afternoon, I got permission from our manager to have a meeting with a professor at school. I went to school and took a seat on a bench within clear visual distance of the door of our faculty, as I waited for Ferda to come out. She was definitely inside and never skipped a lecture. I saw Ferda about half an hour later. She was by herself as she descended quickly down the steps. I guessed I would wait another hour had she dropped into the canteen. That wasn't the case as she headed towards the campus gate. I got up and commenced walking behind her. I greeted a few friends in passing. Telling them I was in a hurry, I exited the campus in order not to let Ferda get away. I walked behind her until the end of the avenue. She went down to Beşiktaş Square and at one stage, removed her backpack and fumbled through it for something. I hid behind a tree in the middle of the sidewalk so she wouldn't see me. From her facial expression, I gathered she didn't find what she was looking for in her bag. When in fact she wasn't the kind of girl who carried her complicated world in her bag… She put the bag back onto her back and continued walking towards Eminönü. I thought she'd wait for a bus at the stop in front of the grilled sheep's intestines shop, but she didn't oblige. I crossed out my plan to board the bus from the rear door. I wondered if she was going to some shopping, but she didn't enter any of the shops either, let alone do any window shopping. She was walking as though she had locked onto a target. I didn't give up on her and would have followed her all the way to Edirne if I had to. It turned out I didn't have to go that distance. My impatience got the better of me when we reached the Maçka turnoff as I ran up to Ferda. I grabbed her arm from behind and turned her around towards me. Thinking I was a mugger, she tried to break free of my grasp. Stopping when she realized it was me, she was stunned.

- Ferda, we've gotta talk.

- No way Sitki, get away from me.

- Whadya mean, no way Ferda, whadya mean, no way?

- Sitki, for God's sake get away from me.

- I'm not going anywhere, Ferda. We're gonna talk.

- I don't want to Sitki, go please.

- Ferda, don't do this to me. Why are you refusing me? We didn't even sit some place outside of school and have a tea for four years.

- I don't want to, Sitki, what happens at school stays at school. Now go away, please.

- Are you playing a game with me? What was it that attracted you to me, what was it made you do everything you could for me to remain attached to you?

- I didn't do anything.

- We're gonna talk now, Ferda. Come and let's sit over there some place.

- Go ahead, fast, get outta here!

If only I'd done what she asked. I should have read the fear in Ferda's eyes and gotten the hell out of there. A fresh resentment was further added to my life when a gray Mercedes-Benz pulled over beside us. Two guys got out of the car, shouting their heads off. One was the driver, the other got out from the rear door and it was clear he was his boss. While the driver stopped spewing obscenities at me to say to Ferda, "Ma'am please get in the car" confirmed my thinking. I couldn't understand what the driver or the boss were saying or why they were swearing. While I stupidly tried asking Ferda what was going on, the boss landed a powerful fist to my jaw. I came eye-to-eye with the bearded boss the instant he landed his blow. I was still conscious and I definitely knew this face from somewhere. He was a guy who appeared on talk programs good for nothing but creating bitter controversy, representing women wearing head scarves and defending polygamy with the manner of an Islamic Army commander defending Jerusalem. The owner of that famous headscarf manufacturer. Yep, it was him alright.

I lost my balance with the force of the fist as I crumpled to the ground. Just then, the driver began hurtling kicks at my head. It was as if an Arabian stallion was stomping over me. The kicks and obscenities rained down incessantly and this thrashing continued for a least five minutes. I heard the boss say, "What do you think you're doing, getting close like that with my wife, you fucking jerk?" I went numb at that moment. I wouldn't have objected or budged a finger even if they drubbed me until eternity. But they didn't continue and it was as if a referee blew the final whistle, as the kicking stopped and the obscenities ceased and detested at once. They got back in their luxury automobile and took off. Of course, Ferda the coldhearted bitch also took off…

Once the guys sped away, quite a few Good Samaritan citizens gathered around me. Though they didn't prevent me from getting beaten up, they did help me to get to my feet. They handed me water and gave me some Kleenex. Blood flowing from my swollen lip had turned my white shirt crimson red. I guess blood that leaked from my head and dyed my chest was my fate. After sitting on the sidewalk for a while, After resting on the sidewalk for a while, I got myself together and stood up. I refused offers for an ambulance and started to walk away. Meanwhile, I was still reeling from the effect of the first fist I was ever struck with in my life. I had a tough time regaining my balance. I turned back and walked to the busstop in front of the grilled sheep's intestines shop. I boarded a bus and went home. Telling mother what had happened took more out of me than the beating I absorbed. That said, the pain of the blows I was struck with manifested itself after I took a shower and laid out on my bed. The guys made me a doughboy and practically steamrolled at a rolling pin over me. I couldn't really get to my feet for almost two days. Thank God there was only the scar of my busted-up lip on my face. My hair camouflaged the scars of the blows to my head. Those motherfuckers were professional rough boys.

Though my bones still ached, I got myself together and went to school on Thursday. The first class was at nine. I don't know why I went so early, but I was at the amphitheater at 08:40. I sat and waited for people to show up. Everyone who arrived looked in my face and wished me a speedy recovery. I was sure they didn't witness the incident. Had they witnessed it, I definitely would've heard it through the grapevine. As they treated me as though I was ill, it meant there was a pain in the blows I suffered to my face. They might have supposed the scar on my lip was a cold sore. Ferdi entered the amphitheater a few minutes prior to the start of class. With the professor behind her... I expected her to come p to me, talk with me and tell me what happened, but I was mistaken again. Ferda looked at my face while passing in front of me.

- Are you ill?

- No. Actually, yes. I'm ill for you, but you don't realize this, and I'm mourning like her mother has died.

Of course I couldn't say anything beyond the 'No.' She wouldn't have heard even if I wanted to say it. Because she walked off before even waiting for an answer to her question. She took in a row at the edge of the window. Just as she looked at my facial expression and asked "Are you ill?" as if it wasn't me who was beaten to within an inch of my life, the fact that she didn't look at my face again really ate me up inside. What was Ferda trying to pull? Would she have gotten a grip had I smacked her one on her dimples? Is that what she wanted from me? She knew I was head over heels in love with her. She was also head over heels in love with me and I knew it as well. Fine, so what was the obstacle between us? Despite getting throttled to within an inch of my life in front of her, what was the obstacle that distanced her from me? Was it true what the boss who swung the first punch? Or else were those words that wandered around in my brain that spun like a cola bottle rattling around from all those kicks and fists just a figment of my imagination? How could they be married? It didn't make any sense because it would take a supercomputer a year to calculate the age difference between the two. I didn't have it in me to ask Ferda. It was left up in the air because she fled again, she always fled. That was the day I knocked on alcohol's door in an effort to find the answer to my question. That habit ended up quite the hospitable guest.

On the drunken nights that I was trailing behind Ferda, I found myself talking to Hatice more and more often. Every single night, words of remorse and rebellion would come pouring out as I struggled to give her an explanation; "I had to pull myself together. Life before death was my right too, wasn't it? Love after you have gone… Maybe that's the reason. So I can forget about you and have a decent love; but no, I couldn't. Once again, I couldn't pull it off. Not that I couldn't forget you. They just wouldn't let me. You know who they are. Just because you left, doesn't mean the country changed. Hatice, just because you died, the monsters who wrote our death sentences didn't die along with you!"

04:25 AM

My nausea subsided and my head was no longer throbbing. I was about to fall fast asleep when I heard a huge noise. As far as I understood from the sound, I guessed a heavy object had fallen near me from above. Something furry also hit the ground right next to my nose at the same moment. I was scared shitless, was it a rat or what! No way, dude, rat don't fall from the sky, do they? That said, I didn't think it was fair when I recalled the tribes that perished merely with the fall of the rain in a country that had bared its bosom to so much evil. But now I was sure that whatever it was next to my nose wasn't a mouse or anything like that. It was both motionless and its fur was really soft... Creeping into my nose, the fur tickled me as I breathed in and out. Perhaps someone dropped their toy from above. Too lazy to budge my hand to itch my nose, I opened my eyes to figure out just what that furry thing which was keeping me from golden slumbers. I encountered pink fur so bright it needed sunglasses at night. And it wasn't a toy either. It's a slipper for fuck's sake! You know, a woman's slipper… Some woman flung it at her husband and it went flying out the window as he ducked out of the way… Great, but were there any homes along this avenue, dickhead? Even if there were, they probably wouldn't be inhabited by anyone else but bitches crazy enough to be flinging slippers onto the street at midnight.

I huffed and puffed at the pink fur so it wouldn't twitch my nose, but to no avail. It invaded my nose as I inhaled deeply. This time I started sneezing. I began hearing the buzz of the crowd. The buzzing came from the spot where I heard that sickening crash the moment the slipper fell next to my head. Some folks were yelling. I wanted to overhear what was said, but I couldn't hear anything as my ears were blocked from my consecutive sneezing. Finally, it dawned on me to budge my hand a bit. I pushed the furry pink slipper away from my nose, giving it some extra comfort. My drowsiness thoroughly dissipated, my body felt feeble, but my consciousness was in relatively good shape compared to when I downed all that beer. I thought I was perceiving sounds better Sesleri and I didn't even have to prick up my ears. Some people were shrieking and a police radio was crackling faintly. As far as I could make out some woman was wailing about something to a police officer who held a walkie-talkie unit. Exclaiming, "I swear officer, he just jumped outta nowhere, we didn't understand what was going on." To my surprise, that sound that deprived me of my slumber belonged to a body that smacked into the ground. While the shrieking woman screamed "Why'd you do it, Ceyda," every so often, the officers began talking amongst themselves. I couldn't quite make an exact determination, but there were at least three officers on the scene. Amongst them, I heard a voice ordering, "Let's check to see if this one's got an I.D. on him somewhere" while another said, "Man, look how she smashed his head on the pavement like that, splattering her brains all over the place." I couldn't differentiate, but perhaps it was the same cop who said, "Sergeant, I found his I.D., it was in his pocket." "Mustafa Narin… registered with the Silvan census bureau…" Considering the name the sergeant read off, the person who smashed into the ground was a male. I was really confused. If this guy committed suicide, maybe someone also tossed him out the window. Great, but what's with the pink slipper? One fell next to my nose, so where was the other one? Besides, why was this woman grieving for someone named Ceyda? The name of the person who hit the ground was Mustafa Narin. Isn't that how the officer read the I.D.? So, what's the deal, dude? My mind is suffering from a momentary lapse of reason.

- I swear, officer, he just suddenly jumped.

- Tell me how he jumped? Why would a person just jump out a window for no reason? What did you do that made him jump?

- I swear, officer, I didn't do anything. There was only the two of us at home.

- Did you take drugs, did you have an argument, go on, what happened?…

- Officer, I swear we weren't arguing and we weren't taking any drugs.

- So, what then happened? Don't piss me off, or else I swear I'll make you talk down at the station. So don't annoy me and tell me what's behind all this?

- Bro, I'm begging you! I swear, we weren't arguing or doing anything else. Ceyda came home around an hour ago bawling her head off. Her mouth and nose were all bruised up. She threw her bag into the living room and stretched out on the couch. I asked her "What happened to you like that." She didn't answer me. I ran to get some ice from the freezer and put some on the bruise above her eye. She refused, grabbing the ice bag and threw it on the ground.

- What happened, didn't she tell you who beat her up?

- She told me, I got it out of her. She made a deal with someone in Harbiye. She got in the guy's car and went to his house. There was someone in the house. They jumped Ceyda the moment she entered the home. They beat the living shit out of the girl, taking whatever she had on her, her money, her phone everything. They emptied her purse and handed it back to her, then they had her get in their car and tossed her out at Balat. She barely had the strength to get in a cab to take her home.

- Then what happened, if she was in fact lying on the couch, why did she jump out the window. These sorts of things always happen to you, You're used to all this. This is nothing new.

- Yes, Ceyda had been feeling really down for quite time now. She kept muttering, I'm going to kill myself and get rid of this life"

- Isn't that what you alway say, you twat! How many of you have jumped from the fifth floor? Why don't all you just jump together and save us all the trouble!

- Bro, I swear! Ceyda's situation was very different. Her mother passed away last month. She was really sad she couldn't return to her homeland, being afraid of her relatives and whatnot. As it was someone did her wrong last night. She was depressed even while she left for work. In fact, I told her, "Don't go to work today, You'll get in a quarrel with customers." She didn't listen to me.

- What happened last night? Who did wrong to whom, what happened?

- Bro, last night, Ceyda visited the home of our friends. Coming out of the home, someone fell in front of her. She said to the guy who fell, "Speedy recovery, are you alright?"

The guy walked off without saying anything. He didn't even look in Ceyda's face.

- Well, so what?

- The guy's attitude really made Ceyda feel pretty awful, officer. You'd turn and look if a dog barked, right? But this guy didn't even stoop to turn around. She talked about this the entire day. As it was, it was the last thing she said while lying out on the couch. She told me, "Defne, we're worth nothing in this shitbag world of ours." The assholes get happy with us and go home to sleep with their wives. The guys we wish a speedy recovery to don't even look in our faces, Defne. They just know how to step all over us, that's all. I'm going to step all over this fucking life, Defne," as she cried sobbingly. Blood seeped from her bruised eye, officer. Then she suddenly got to her feet and went into her room. I followed her from behind. I leaned against her door and watched to see what she was doing. She opened her wardrobe closet bent over and and pulled out a pair of slippers from under the closet. One of them was split open on the side, but Ceyda loved those pink slippers, officer. Officer, did you know she threw those slippers down a well when she was back at home. She couldn't bear it later on, she tied a rope around her waist and went down into the well. The slippers were floating on the water. She removed them at the risk of drowning. Ever since that day, she hid them like a treasure. She put the slippers on where she sat, then she got to her feet and closed the closet doors. Then she just stood there a little. I asked her, "What happened,

Ceyda girl, what are you thinking about," but she didn't say anything. She suddenly turned around, shoved me aside as I fell to the floor and sauntered towards the living room. I got up quickly and ran after her to the living room. She flew the curtain aside and opened the window, officer. She looked outside a bit, then turned to me, and said, "Instead of fleeing from my hometown, if only I had thrown myself down the well with these slippers. If only we were buried together at the bottom of the well. Then from there to the depths of Hell…" I swear, She was breathing from her nose. She took off her slippers and threw them out the window. I understood she was going to jump, but I couldn't get to her in time. She jumped out, saying, "Now you can wish me a speedy recovery," officer. What am I going to do now, man? "What did you do, Ceyda! Why did you do this, why did you do this!"

Goddamn me. Fuck, what kinda shit did I find myself in? Shit, for years, I cursed at those around me because they weren't part of the civilized world and I'm the cause of someone's suicide for abstaining two words. Notwithstanding, from what I overheard, apparently there were reasons greater than my dickheadedness for her jumping out of the window. Then again, had I said, "Thanks," that might've done miracles for the poor woman. Fuck, she might even still be alive today. I better get up and get the fuck away from here before the CSI team arrives on the scene. They could scrutinize the slipper in front of me and label me as the murderer. It might have potential to be appreciated, but it doesn't resemble the moral compass of a set of police handcuffs. One links to peace, the other to the police station holding tank.

I don't know if it counted as tampering with evidence, but not wanting to find myself in hot water, I thrust the pink furry slipper into my jacket pocket. The heel was stuck outside, but hey, it's all good. As I was able to carry out this rapid endeavor, it meant I had the strength to get up from my place. First, I got to my knees and turned my head a bit. I opened two buttons of my shirt collar and got to my feet after breathing in a while. The cops were still interrogating suicide Mustafa Narin's roommate on the street. I didn't look in that direction as I turned around and walked off. I increased my pace as I got further away. I threw my left hand onto my chest and pressed tightly so the slipper didn't fall from my pocket. I didn't turn down the first street so as not to attract attention. I walked a bit further at a faster pace. After believing I got quite away from the scene, I dove into darkness the first chance I had. I went to the bottom of the Street and came out in Tarlabaşı. I was about to be mowed down by a car as I passed over to the other side of the boulevard. The driver swerved at the last moment as he sent a blast of obscenities my way. He was right, I couldn't say anything. I sat on the sidewalk with my left hand still on my chest. I took out the slipper and hesitated whether to toss it into the trash container just up the way or not. I said no way as I was still close to the crime scene. I should eliminate the slipper someplace far from here. I was like a criminal trying to eliminate evidence. I looked at my watch, it was 5 o' clock. The sun was going to come up pretty soon. I've got half an hour. To what? To prayer time, of course. I got up, and got in the cab waiting in front of the line for a fare. I said, "Take me to Eyüp, bro." He said, "Okay," and stepped on the gas. We passed over to Unkapanı and turned off towards Balat. After moving a while, the cabbies asked, "Which one are you going to." Which one? I gave him a sleazy look as I eyed me in his rearview mirror. This time he asked, "Are you going to have sheep's head and foot soup, which soup shop shall I drop you off at?"

- No man, what soup shop? We're going to the Eyüp Mosque.

- To the mosque?

- Yeah man, to the mosque. Let's pick it up a bit, it's almost time.

- Alright, let's go to the mosque.

Setting out with the assumption he'd be dropping off a drunkard who hung out at a beerhouse until morning at a soup joint, the cabbie said, "Okay, let's go t the mosque," as he gave me a cynical expression. We passed the Feshane and turned at the intersection. The cab stopped on the avenue on the upper side of Eyüp Sultan Mosque. I reached my right hand into my trouser pocket, took out some money and handed it to the cabbie. He still had that cynical smirk on his face when he gave me my change. I thought for a moment not to take the change, but his sarcastic looks made me change my mind. It was as if the cunt never had a hangover. I got out of the cab and didn't close the door completely out of spite. I want him to stop and get out when he realized the door was open. As I walked from the square towards the mosque, I tossed the slipper in my pocket into the first trash container I encountered. After taking a few steps, I turned back and fetched the slipper from the trash container and promptly stuck it back into my jacket pocket. The slipper wasn't safe, they could find it here as well. There were cameras everywhere. I ended up more of paranoiac than the police I couldn't ignore the possibility of tracking me down. What was the big deal about lying down in front of that building. As though there wasn't any other place to pass the fuck out.

While stepping into the mosque courtyard, I straightened up my mouth. I was going to care of the furry slipper after prayer services. The best thing to do waas to walk down to the shore and fling it into the Golden Horn. I went over to the ablutions fountain, which wasn't very crowded as it was a weekday. It would've been a circus had it been Sunday. I removed my jacket and hung it up, keeping the slipper out of sight. After taking off my watch and sticking it in my trouser pocket, I rolled up the sleeves of my white shirt.I noticed my sleeve cuffs were jet black. It must have been from dragging my arms on the concrete while lying on the ground... I turned on the tap and was hit with remarkably bracing cold water for a summer's day. I did my ablutions. I don't remember if I may have missed some religious duties.

After putting on my shoes, I stood up and put my jacket back on. I rubbed my hands on my face to wipe away the drops of water. At that moment, the midnight photographer with the head scarf came to mind. I looked at my right hand, the numbers were faint... Let's face it, I was unlucky?

I stuck my right hand as well as the rubbed out telephone number which had clouded up my sober mind, into my pocket and began walking over to the mosque. A wormy thought entered my mind in front of the door. "Dude, I'd been drinking. Can one pray while under the influence? It wasn't like that before, dude, it was supposed to be you don't pray if you're under the influence. What difference was there? I don't know if there was any difference, but I'm not drunk at the moment." The worm got the best of me as I should have picked the morning of a day I didn't swim in a bottle of alcohol if I wanted to conduct prayer services. As it was, the Eyüp congregation, which according to other mosques conducts its service just prior to dawn, had slowly started to emerge outside. The sun was on the verge of rising. Those who donned their shoes were heading over to the tomb. I shouldn't get mixed up in that lot.

Then again, I was anxious. Like a wine bottle waiting to be kicked to smithereens in the mosque courtyard... When in fact, I preferred to sleep in the bosom of a drunkard. Neither the wine which Allah has forbidden would have come to mind, nor could I have lived with the fear of being shattered to bits with the kick of a pious Moslem. If only I had the privilege of choosing which one…

 **Onder Deligoz** graduated from Istanbul University's Department of Journalism and has worked as a reporter, editor and director in various newspapers and television since 2004. The author has many researches, written texts, and documentary texts on political and social events related to Turkey's recent history. *Love After You Have Gone* is the authors first novel. The book has met readers around the world in both Turkish and English.